To Nowhere and Back

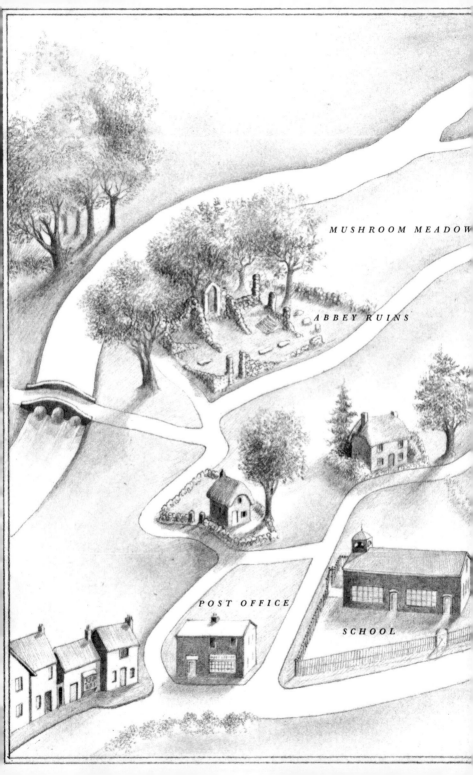

MUSHROOM MEADOW

ABBEY RUINS

POST OFFICE

SCHOOL

TO SPRINGFIELD FARM

ANN'S COTTAGE

RANDOM COTTAGE

OLD GRAVEYARD

TO MERSTON →

Illustration by Laszlo Kubinyi

To Nowhere and Back

ঽ ঙ

MARGARET J. ANDERSON

Alfred A. Knopf New York

For Susan and Karen

This is a Borzoi Book published by Alfred A. Knopf, Inc.

Copyright © 1975 by Margaret Anderson.
All rights reserved under International and Pan-American Copyright
Conventions. Published in the United States by Alfred A. Knopf, Inc.,
New York, and simultaneously in Canada by Random House of Can-
ada Limited, Toronto. Distributed by Random House, Inc., New York.

Library of Congress Cataloging in Publication Data
Anderson, Margaret J. To nowhere and back.
SUMMARY: Elizabeth, an avowed realist, finds herself able to move in
and out of the mind and body of a girl who lived one hundred years
earlier.
[1. Space and time—Fiction.] I. Kubinyi, Laszlo, 1937– illus. II. Title.
PZ7.A54397To [Fic] 74–16335 ISBN 0–394–83036–9 ISBN 0–394–93036–3
(lib. bdg.)

Designed by Cathy Goldsmith
Manufactured in the United States of America
2 4 6 8 0 9 7 5 3

Contents

1   Random Cottage   1

2   Waterberry School   10

3   The Cottages   23

4   Castles and Mansions   31

5   Ann   39

6   Scrubber Liz   46

7   Michael   58

8   New Friends   70

9   Potato Picking   82

10   Visitors   91

11   The Lucky Bonnet   101

12   The Mushroom Meadow   117

13   The Shawl   128

14   Back to Nowhere   135

To Nowhere and Back

≥ 1 ≤

Random Cottage

Wedged in the back seat of the small Morris between two suitcases and a picnic basket, Elizabeth listened to her parents discussing whether they should have turned right or left at the crossroads. Her mother had said to turn left, but now her father thought they should have turned right.

"See if you can find this village on the map," Mr. Fenner suggested to his wife.

"It's called Lower Waterberry," said Elizabeth over her father's shoulder. "Couldn't we stop here for a coke? It looks historic." She added the historic part because her parents were much more interested in history than coke.

Rather to Elizabeth's surprise, Mr. Fenner brought the car to a sudden stop outside the village post office and said, "All right. I'll take a look at the map while you two stretch your legs."

Elizabeth went into the post office, which also

1

served as a general store, and bought her coke. Her mother followed her into the little shop and stood reading a number of notices taped to the glass door.

"Listen to this, Elizabeth! For Rent: Random Cottage. Small furnished cottage with view. Close to school and shops. Reasonable rates."

"Are you people looking for a furnished house?" asked the postmistress, coming out from behind the counter.

"Yes, we are," said Elizabeth's mother, and was soon explaining that Mr. Fenner was on a year's leave from a college in Timberhill, Oregon, where he taught history and literature. He was interested in Thomas Hardy—the writer who had lived around here a hundred years ago—and that had brought them to Dorset. Now they were looking for a place to stay near Dorchester, where he could do research and reading. Then Mrs. Fenner went on to say that she, herself, wrote books but she could do that anywhere. And they must find somewhere close to a good school for Elizabeth.

Elizabeth shuffled uncomfortably, feeling that it was hardly necessary for her mother to tell their whole life story to a perfect stranger. But the postmistress was more than interested and was soon telling them all about the village and arranging for them to see the cottage.

When Mr. Fenner heard about the cottage, he

agreed it would be a fine location. "I've found Lower Waterberry on the map, and we are quite close to Dorchester here."

"And there is where Elizabeth would go to school," said her mother, pointing to a red brick building further along the road. "The postmistress assures me that it's a very good school."

Elizabeth looked at the building with a scowl. The windows were small and high, and there was a forbidding look about the worn steps leading up to the narrow entrances with "Boys" chiseled in stone above one and "Girls" above the other. She could imagine a tall, stern teacher, with a cane in his hand, standing behind a high desk.

Perhaps it was the thought of school, but Elizabeth could not share her parents' enthusiasm about the idea of settling down in England. While the postmistress was busy making arrangements for her sister, Mrs. Higgins, to show them the house, Elizabeth found herself hoping it wouldn't be suitable.

When Mrs. Higgins arrived, it was easy to see that she was afraid that the Fenners, being from America, would find the cottage too inconvenient and old-fashioned. Her ideas of American family life were based on TV and the movies. Elizabeth could have told her not to worry. As far as her parents were concerned everything improved with age—an opinion Elizabeth did not share.

But when they turned up the steep, winding lane, just beyond the school, and found the little white cottage with its thick, thatched roof, sitting snug against the hillside, even Elizabeth was excited.

Mrs. Higgins unlocked the door and ushered them in. At first the rooms seemed dim in contrast to the brightness outside. The windows were small, but in the dining room, a patch of sun brightened the blue plates and brass kettles on the large oak sideboard. There was a round, polished table, and the ladderback chairs had worn red velvet seats.

The furniture, like the house, was sturdy and old and comfortable. A big grandfather clock stood in the corner by the stairs, and two easy chairs were arranged by the fireplace in the sitting room.

Mrs. Higgins told them that the cottage was over two hundred years old. The kitchen and bathroom had been added at a much later date, though when Elizabeth looked at the appliances and bathroom fixtures, she decided it hadn't been *that* much later.

Upstairs were two large bedrooms with oak beams running crookedly across the ceiling. Plaster was flaking here and there from the whitewashed walls. In one bedroom the far wall curved outward, and then sloped back toward the roof. Elizabeth thought that perhaps the builder had not had a tool for measuring angles, but later found that this was the chimney from the downstairs fireplace.

"Imagine! Two hundred years of history in this

house," said Mr. Fenner. "Just think of all the families that have lived here before us. It's the people that lived on the land, in cottages like this, that wrote the history of England. History isn't kings and parliaments and great cathedrals. It's the little people, the villagers, the townspeople. . . ."

"That's very true, sir!" said Mrs. Higgins agreeably. "Now, about the rent in advance. . ."

Elizabeth ran downstairs and outside. She could see that living in a house like this was going to give her father a lot of opportunities to turn life into one long history lesson. Her parents claimed that she had no imagination because she didn't get excited about ruins and abbeys and antiques. But why spend all your time thinking about what happened two hundred years ago when there is so much happening right now?

True to her philosophy, Elizabeth switched her thoughts to the present. The garden would be good for hide-and-seek, and there were trees to climb. In front of the house was a small lawn surrounded by borders of lupins and delphiniums and roses. To the side, separated from the lawn by a trimmed hedge, was a wild garden.

Elizabeth pushed through the hedge into this densely overgrown garden. Flowering currant, with its catty smell, tangled with the brittle fingers of a forsythia bush. Lank grass and nettles grew everywhere. A cherry tree reached up above the bushes and Elizabeth swung herself onto a stout lower limb. She was soon high enough to see over the bushes and over the ragged boundary hedge, too. The ground fell away steeply, so that she looked down on the roofs and chimney pots of a row of houses on the Merston Road below. Beyond were fields, trees, and hedges—the patchwork quilt of the English countryside.

"Elizabeth! Elizabeth!"

Mr. Fenner's voice penetrated the sanctuary of the treetop.

"Coming, Dad," answered Elizabeth, and appeared at the front door a few minutes later with a leaf in her light brown hair and mud stains on her socks.

Her parents were unloading the car.

"We're going to move in! Take these books into the front room, Elizabeth," said her mother. "And then you can unpack your suitcase."

Elizabeth walked into the sitting room and laid the books down on the windowsill. As she did so she suddenly had a strange feeling that she was being watched. She turned around quickly, but there was no one there. Yet the feeling persisted that she was not alone.

Mrs. Higgins had gone back down to the village, and she could hear her parents talking to each other outside. Elizabeth took a long, slow look around the empty room, shrugged, and hurried back outside.

"Which will my bedroom be?" she asked, grabbing her suitcase.

"Upstairs, turn left," answered her father.

Elizabeth clattered upstairs. She noticed that the doors were oddly shaped, cut to fit the sloping roof. Little metal latches held the doors closed.

Elizabeth lifted the latch and went in. She crossed the room and opened the small window. The walls were so thick that the windowsill formed a seat, and from there she could lean out and touch the bristly, cut ends of the thatch. It gives the house a bushy-eyebrow look, she thought.

Below her was a fat box hedge. It was trimly clipped and looked as solid and bouncy as a mattress. Elizabeth considered jumping from the window onto it but decided against it. Her parents were in sight and would surely forbid her ever to do it again, and she might want to. If, for instance, the house caught fire.

"Dad," she called. "Don't you think this kind of roof is dangerous? It could easily catch on fire."

"You're right," answered her father. "But this house has stood for two hundred years without anyone being careless with fire, and we'll have to be careful, too!"

Elizabeth drew her head back in the window.

"Two hundred years!" she muttered. "There we go again!"

She jumped up and touched the ceiling. Some flakes of plaster fell with a little pattering sound. She swept them guiltily under the bed and found herself hoping that the house would last for two hundred and one years.

Elizabeth opened her suitcase and began to put her belongings haphazardly into drawers. She propped up last year's class picture beside her mirror and laid her diary beside her bed. She really should start to keep the diary, she thought guiltily. It had been a present from her best friend, Monica, back in Timberhill.

She opened it and wrote:

September 1. We found a cottage today. It's called "Random." Dad says we've been living at random for weeks (joke). We're going to stay in one place now so that I can go to school.

Elizabeth stopped writing and stared out of the window. School. . . How she dreaded the thought of going to a new school! She would have to wear some silly uniform, but that wasn't what worried her most. Suppose these English girls didn't like her? She had tried to tell her parents how she felt, but her mother had only said, "You'll make friends all right." And her father had added, "They'll be interested to meet someone new." But Elizabeth didn't think that was the way it worked out. She'd be new, and she'd be different. She remembered how she and her friends

8

had treated that new girl, Virginia, last year; they hadn't even tried to be nice to her. And now it was her turn to be Virginia.

She sighed and then slammed the diary shut and went down to see if her parents had brought themselves back to the present sufficiently to think about preparing supper.

❧ 2 ❧
Waterberry School

It seemed to Elizabeth that for the next few days all they talked about was school. There was a trip into Dorchester to buy clothes, and Elizabeth was outfitted with a gray, pleated skirt, a blue sweater, a white shirt, and a striped tie. She didn't like the idea of being dressed exactly like everyone else but at the same time worried that her clothes might somehow be different.

Then she and her mother visited the school. Elizabeth decided it was even worse close up—all that drab green paint along the corridors. But the office was bright and cheerful, and the principal was very friendly. Mrs. Fenner described him later as "young and progressive," but Elizabeth knew better than to judge a teacher by how he appeared to parents.

"We'll see you tomorrow," he said to Elizabeth as they left. "You'll go to Mr. Ranton's room at the end of the hall."

So the next morning, Elizabeth and her mother again walked down the lane from Random Cottage to the main road. Elizabeth kicked at some loose stones, scuffing her new brown oxfords.

"Walk properly, Elizabeth," her mother said in an irritated voice.

Elizabeth looked up at her mother and wondered if she, too, was nervous about the school. But she doesn't have to go there every day, thought Elizabeth, giving a big stone a fierce kick.

When they reached the main road, they could see the school at their end of the village. Beyond it were the post office and a few shops and cottages. Then, farther on, was the Housing Scheme—a sprawl of small, boxlike houses each with a little garden patch. Great numbers of children were coming from the Housing Scheme towards school.

"You'll find Mr. Ranton's room, all right?" Mrs. Fenner asked a little anxiously.

"Sure," answered Elizabeth and leaving her mother, she merged with the throng of children pushing through the playground gate.

A loud bell clanged, and excited children ran to form lines at the two doors—little children at one and bigger children at the other, and not "Boys" and "Girls" as the doors proclaimed.

Elizabeth joined the line of older children a little uncertainly. Next to her stood a girl with long fair bangs. Flicking her hair back from her eyes, the girl turned to Elizabeth and asked, "Whose class are you in?"

"Mr. Ranton's," answered Elizabeth.

"Good! I am, too—except we call him Rant-'n-Rave. You'll soon see why."

This didn't sound reassuring.

"I'm Nancy Pearson. You can sit by me if you like."

"Oh, yes, I would like to," answered Elizabeth. They walked in line down the dim corridor, talking together, and Elizabeth didn't even notice the drab green paint today, she was so pleased to have Nancy beside her.

Their classroom was a bright new room that had been added to the school and had big windows and a door to the playground. The double desks were arranged in rows facing the blackboard. The teacher was sitting at his desk. He had gray hair, and his glasses had slipped down to the end of his nose. He looked up, surprised by all the noise and confusion. It was almost as if he hadn't expected school to start so soon.

Nancy sprawled over a double desk.

"Sit here by me," she said to Elizabeth.

"Hey, Nancy, are you saving me a seat?" said a tall girl from the doorway.

"It's for Elizabeth," said Nancy, uncertainly.

"But I always sit beside you," said the other girl.

"You can sit in front, Mandy," said Nancy, but children were already scrambling for the desks in front.

Mandy turned, tossing her long blond braids, and marched to the front of the room and sat with another girl.

Elizabeth looked around at the roomful of blue sweaters and felt she'd never be able to sort everyone out. The desk lids banged as the children thrust their lunches inside and pulled out small blue books.

"Back in Timberhill, Oregon, we had lockers for our books and things," said Elizabeth.

The teacher rapped on his desk for silence and then called out the names from the register.

"Line up at the door," barked Mr. Ranton, and once again there was confusion in the room.

"Where are we going?" Elizabeth asked.

"Down to the hall for prayers," answered Nancy.

"Back in Oregon we couldn't have prayers in school," said Elizabeth.

"Imagine that!" said Mandy, who was beside them again in the reshuffle as they lined up at the door.

"You can share my hymnbook," Nancy said to Elizabeth.

"But I was going to share with you," broke in Mandy.

Walking down the corridor to the hall, Mandy pushed in next to Nancy, and Elizabeth was without a partner. She felt a little left out. And then when they returned to the classroom and started lessons, everyone but Elizabeth seemed to have books and papers and work to do.

She sat at her empty desk hoping that Mr. Ranton would soon notice that she had no books. It surprised her to see everyone else so busy. Back in Timberhill you could count on most of the first week of school being spent in getting organized. That way you really knew you'd had a vacation.

At last Mr. Ranton called her up to his desk and handed her several textbooks and exercise books and told her to read the first chapter in the history book.

However, a bell rang before she had even found the page. It was time for recess—playtime, they called it.

The children poured out of the classrooms. Different sizes of children migrated to different areas of the playground, observing invisible barriers of long standing. There was a large area of black top and a sloping field.

Elizabeth looked at the bare playground surrounded by its high fence. "Back in Timberhill, Oregon, we have twirling bars and a slide and swings in our playground. I once twirled seventy-five times," said Elizabeth.

Nobody answered.

Elizabeth, herself, didn't realize that almost every time she spoke she started out with, "Back in Timberhill, Oregon. . ." It was just that everything here was different, and she was ill at ease, missing the things she was used to. But to the children at Lower Waterberry Primary School it sounded as if Elizabeth was criticizing their school. They spent a lot of time doing that themselves, but no newcomer could get away with it.

"Let's skip," said Mandy. The rope turned, and the girls ran in and out to the rhythm of a jingle. Elizabeth waited her turn nervously and then missed the beat and got tangled in the rope.

"Back in Timberhill, Oregon, they don't turn the rope so fast," said Mandy, imitating Elizabeth's accent and making the girls laugh.

Elizabeth, red-faced and close to tears, turned away from the skipping game.

The boys were playing soccer in the field. Elizabeth went over and watched them without really seeing the game. One boy headed the ball, and it soared over the wire fence and bounced across the road. The boys ran to the fence and stood in a row, staring out at the lost ball. Like caged sheep, thought Elizabeth spitefully.

"I'll get it for you," she shouted.

The boys turned and stared at her. Nobody said

anything, so Elizabeth marched across the playground, unbolted the gate, and ran out to retrieve the ball.

She was picking it up when a shrill whistle blew. The clamor in the playground slowly subsided, and when Elizabeth turned around, she found everyone looking at her.

"Come here, girl!" shouted the teacher who had blown the whistle.

Elizabeth walked through the silent children and slowly approached the teacher. Her face was scarlet, and she was again close to tears. The teacher took the soccer ball from her hands and tossed it over to the waiting boys.

Elizabeth looked up at the teacher. She wore a heavy tweed coat and had a wool head-scarf tied over her gray hair.

She looked down at Elizabeth and said, quite kindly, "You're new?"

Elizabeth nodded.

"Can't have you running into the street after balls. School rule."

"Then how do they get the ball back?" asked Elizabeth.

"Look over there, and you'll see," said the teacher.

The ball had again bounced over the fence, and the boys crowded to the wire.

"Please, miss! Please, miss!" they shouted to a

stout lady, who was puffing along with her heavy shopping baskets.

The lady set down the baskets, waddled into the road, and heaved the ball back over the wire fence. She stood beaming at the children for a few minutes and then picked up her baskets and puffed on her way.

"You'll get used to us," said the teacher to Elizabeth, with a friendly smile.

A bell rang summoning the children back to their classes. Elizabeth followed a group of girls back to her room and felt that she'd never fit in with all these busy, blue-sweatered children. The day was ruled by bells and barked orders. Everyone always knew what would happen next, except Elizabeth. She was always two steps behind and nobody cared.

Finally the last bell of the day rang, and the children spilled out of the classroom in a noisy, excited throng.

"How was school, dear?" her mother asked, when Elizabeth came home.

"It was awful—awful," said Elizabeth, and the tears she'd been holding back all day poured down her cheeks.

Her mother was taken aback. She had expected Elizabeth to burst in full of enthusiasm for her new school and friends. "Let's have a cup of tea and then go for a walk," she said. "We don't even need to talk about school unless you want to."

Her mother kept her word and didn't question Elizabeth about what was wrong with school. Instead they went exploring.

A little way down the lane was a gate leading into a field. They cut across the field, skirted the graveyard around the church, and then followed a footpath across another field.

"This path is a 'right-of-way'," explained her mother. "The farmers have always allowed people to cross these fields, and even when they plough, they leave a strip along the path."

"Where does it go?" asked Elizabeth.

"I've only followed it as far as the woods," answered her mother. "I suppose there were once cottages there, and this was the way people came to Lower Waterberry."

"Let's go into the woods," suggested Elizabeth. "There's a stile over the fence."

Elizabeth led the way over the stile.

The path on the other side was overgrown with weeds, and they had to push their way into the woods through the low branches of hazel trees. Further into the wood the path became more distinct, and there was more open area than they had expected.

"It looks as if they are replanting trees," said Mrs. Fenner, pointing out some young fir trees.

"Maybe we could cut a Christmas tree here," suggested Elizabeth.

"I doubt it. These woods belong to somebody. Probably Springfield Farm. It's all right to walk through them, but we couldn't cut the trees."

The fir trees were just about eight or ten feet high, and the wood was pleasantly open. Stitchwort and vetch grew by the path in a pretty tangle of white and purple. Sparrows bickered on a nearby branch.

They came to a fork in the path.

"Which way?" asked her mother.

Elizabeth picked two stems of grass and, concealing the ends from her mother, said, "Short we go left, long we go right."

Her mother drew the long stem so they followed the path to the right. Birds sang and brown and blue butterflies danced ahead of them.

They had almost reached the far edge of the wood when they came upon two tumbledown cottages in a clearing. Their thatched roofs were rotted so that, in places, you could see the supporting beams. Moss grew on the thatch, and here and there weeds sprouted untidily through the roof. In places the walls were crumbling.

They walked around to the front, and although it

was obvious that the cottages were empty, they walked quietly as if they might be trespassing on someone's garden.

From the front, the cottages looked even more derelict. They were built together, sharing a common wall. The windows stared out like sightless eyes, and one door hung partly open. The brambles had grown around the door so that it would neither open wider nor close.

"Could we go in?" asked Elizabeth.

"I suppose so," answered her mother. "But do be careful, Elizabeth."

Elizabeth pushed her way in. The air had a dank smell, and it was dark inside the house after coming in from the sunshine. The floor was partly covered with linoleum, which had cracked and rotted near the door to expose flat flagstones. There was wallpaper with a busy design of roses and birds, but it was stained with damp and mold. Here and there it had peeled loose to expose blue wallpaper decorated with forget-me-nots and daisies.

Against one wall were several bales of straw in an untidy pile.

Elizabeth went into the next room. It was much like the first, but there was a staircase against the back wall.

"Can I go upstairs, Mother?" asked Elizabeth.

"No, dear! The floorboards may be rotten."

"I'll be careful," said Elizabeth.

"No!" her mother answered again.

Elizabeth wandered back into the first room and climbed around on the bales of straw. She felt vaguely dissatisfied with the place. There was really nothing to do or to see once you did get inside.

"It's sad to think that this was once someone's home. Think of the meals cooked over this fire and the pride of the person who put on the new wallpaper," mused Mrs. Fenner.

"I like the blue stuff better," said Elizabeth carelessly. "Let's get out of here. There's nothing to see."

"But don't these old walls give you a feel of the past?" asked her mother. "This would be a good setting for a story."

"Whose house do you think it was?" asked Elizabeth. She wasn't especially interested, but her mother seemed to want to talk about the place.

"I suppose these cottages were built for farm laborers. But now that farmers have tractors and combine harvesters and such, they don't need laborers living in cottages on their farms."

"But they could rent the cottages to someone," suggested Elizabeth.

"I don't expect anyone wants to live this far from the village. It's really an isolated spot."

"Can we look inside the other cottage?" asked Elizabeth.

21

"Just take a quick look and then we must start for home," answered her mother. "Dad will be there already, and he'll be wondering where we have disappeared to."

However, the door of the second cottage was swollen shut, so Elizabeth and her mother started back down the path through the woods.

❧ 3 ❧
The Cottages

Elizabeth sat at the breakfast table, frowning at a bowl of cereal. She pushed a spoon around but did not eat.

"I don't want to go to school," she said.

"Don't you feel well?" her mother asked.

"I'm okay. It's just school. I'm not going."

"Elizabeth, if you're not sick, you *have* to go," her mother answered in an exasperated voice. "Staying away will only make it harder for you."

It was Friday morning, the fourth day of school. The other days had not been as bad as the first, but Elizabeth was still not happy there.

"I could study at home," she suggested eagerly. "You and Dad could teach me lots. I could help him with his research."

"You know how interested you are in that," answered her mother. "Look, Dad will be home early this afternoon. We'll go down to the sea just as soon as you get home from school. Maybe we could even buy that little shell-lady you liked at the Merston Bay giftshop."

This was a bribe and they both knew it. Just the week before they had been at the giftshop and Elizabeth had asked her mother to buy the ornament. It was an old-fashioned lady made of shells. Her skirt was formed from overlapping scallop shells, and her face was painted on a cockle shell. Her mother had said that it was "tourist rubbish" and that the shells weren't even local shells. So Elizabeth had said she'd buy it with her own money and then had found that she hadn't enough.

She wasn't sure that she wanted the shell-lady any more, but she did like going down to the beach. Also, she knew she'd have to go to school in the end, so she might as well agree to the plan.

School wasn't so bad that Friday. It was library day, and although the library only consisted of two shelves of books loaned from the County Library, Elizabeth found a good book for herself. She pointed out a book to Nancy that she was sure she'd like, and they whispered together about their favorite books until Mr. Ranton shouted for silence.

As they were leaving school, Nancy asked, "Can you come over and play with me?"

"I can't today," answered Elizabeth. "My Dad is taking us to Merston Bay the minute I get home from school."

Elizabeth ran home. A thin drizzle of rain was falling, but Elizabeth was light-hearted. Nancy was friendly, the weekend had come at last, and she was going down to the beach with her parents.

"Hi! I hurried home," shouted Elizabeth, as she burst into the house.

"Oh, Elizabeth, I'm sorry!" said her mother, looking up from her book. "Dad called from Dorchester to say he'd found some interesting old records in the County Courthouse. He wants to go on working on them, and he thought that since the weather has turned nasty you wouldn't want to go to the beach."

"It's hardly even raining, and I like it at the beach when there's nobody else there," said Elizabeth in a disappointed voice.

"I am sorry, my dear!" said her mother. Then she asked, "Before you take your coat off, would you go down to the baker's and get me a loaf of bread? I had planned to stop there on the way to Merston. And buy some of those little cakes you like, and we'll have tea."

She handed Elizabeth some money, and Elizabeth set off down the lane again. She bought the loaf and then spent some time choosing the cakes.

Outside the baker's shop she met Nancy and Mandy.

"Nancy told me you were much too busy to play with her," sneered Mandy.

Elizabeth wanted to explain that her father hadn't

come home. It would have been quite easy if Mandy hadn't been there. Instead she said nothing. She turned and marched off up the road, the loaf wrapped in flimsy, flapping tissue paper in one hand, and her little bag of cakes in the other.

By the time she reached home she was furious with everyone—her father for putting off their drive, her mother for sending her to the baker's, Nancy for gossiping about her, and Mandy for being Mandy.

"There's your cakes!" she said to her mother. "I'm going out for a walk. It's not too wet for me to go to the store, so it's not too wet for a walk."

"All right, dear," said her mother mildly. She knew Elizabeth well enough not to try to coax her out of a bad mood. "Why don't you take your cake and eat it on the way?"

Elizabeth had no idea where she wanted to go, so she set off down the lane. She was soon following the path she and her mother had taken on Tuesday. It was then that she thought of the deserted cottages and decided she'd go to them again. This time she'd get into the other cottage. She'd go upstairs, too.

Elizabeth was not especially curious about the cottages. She wasn't hoping to find a secret treasure or somebody's lost diary in an upstairs room. She just felt contrary, and because the last time her mother had forbidden her to go upstairs, that's exactly what she'd do today.

There were no butterflies along the path, and the wet weeds brushed coldly against her legs. The rain had almost stopped, and the damp earth in the woods smelled fresh and good. A thrush was trilling a joyful song while pigeons cooed in sad undertones.

Elizabeth reached the fork in the path, and just as she started down the right branch, she noticed that the wood was darker and denser than she remembered it. Instead of small fir trees, she was walking through a grove of beech and elm and lime. The branches of the trees met over her head, cutting out the light. It was strange she hadn't noticed these big trees last time. The path was well trodden and ended abruptly at the clearing where the cottages stood.

Here things seemed different, too. The clearing was bigger, and an area was planted out in potatoes and cabbages. There were two beehives that hadn't been there before. They were funny little hives like small igloos made out of basketwork. Skeps, she believed they were called. Her father must have told her that.

There was a strange atmosphere about the place that she hadn't been aware of the other day. It was as if the very trees were holding their branches still, waiting for her to come. She was almost afraid to look at the houses, for she knew that they were waiting, too.

Then she turned toward them and saw that the

decayed thatch was replaced with thick, new straw. The crumbling walls were intact. Smoke curled from each chimney, and although the garden was untidy, it showed signs of care.

Elizabeth stood in puzzled wonder for a long time. The waiting silence frightened her, but she forced herself to skirt around the clearing so that she could see the front of the houses. Curtains hung in the windows, and the doors of both cottages were closed.

There was a jumble of small sheds that she hadn't seen before. One was a chicken house, and several hens scratched around among the chickweed and groundsel in a small pen.

Elizabeth suddenly remembered the time when she was very small and had been taken to see the play, *Hansel and Gretel*. She stood looking at the cottages, feeling that they were pulling her close the way the little candy house had bewitched Hansel and Gretel. Then one of the cottage doors flew open, and Elizabeth drew a sharp breath and her heart skipped a beat. The swinging door was the first movement in the silent, waiting clearing.

She was surprised to see a girl come out of the cottage carrying a bucket. She wore a faded ragged dress, which reached almost to her feet. A brown wool shawl covered her shoulders, and a little round white cap perched on her unruly black hair. Standing in the doorway, framed by the fading roses, she reminded Elizabeth of a picture she'd seen of children long ago.

The girl closed the door behind her and skipped lightly across the grass. Elizabeth stood transfixed, but the girl walked toward the hen run without seeing her. She tossed the contents of the bucket over the fence. The hens ran squawking as the shower of scraps landed among them and then began to peck hungrily at the food. The girl laid down the bucket and undid the fence. Pushing down a post, she clambered in. She stooped low and disappeared into the henhouse. In a few minutes she reappeared holding several eggs in her bunched skirts. Carefully, she pushed her way out of the hen run, transferred the eggs to the bucket, and then fastened the fence again.

Elizabeth made no attempt to hide and stood watching every movement of the thin, ragged child. On her way back to the cottage the girl saw Elizabeth, and they stared at each other. The strange girl had dirty, bare feet and thin, brown arms. Her face was small and elflike, and her hair was thick and dark and tangled. Her eyes were huge and she gazed steadily at Elizabeth. Then she smiled suddenly, showing small, even teeth.

Before Elizabeth had time to speak, the girl turned and walked back to the cottage. Just before the door closed Elizabeth heard the shrill clamor of children's voices and a deeper voice calling them to come and eat. Then the door slammed, shutting off the sounds from Elizabeth. She had expected the girl to turn around and stood waiting for her to come out again, but nothing more happened.

She was sure she must have seemed strange to the child, yet the girl had only looked and smiled. No surprise, no questions, just a quick smile.

Elizabeth stood for a minute longer. Had she really been here before—was she really here now? She turned and ran through the dark woods. Gradually, the big trees gave way to the more open woodland. The birds sang and the flowers glistened with rain-drops, but Elizabeth saw nothing except the narrow path that would take her home.

She ran till her breath was short and her side ached, and still she ran. Out of the woods and across the fields. Up the lane to her own house.

Her mother came out of the kitchen and smiled to Elizabeth.

"There you are, dear," she said. "Where have you been?"

"Nowhere," answered Elizabeth, and then had the uncomfortable feeling that she spoke the truth.

≫ 4 ≪
Castles and Mansions

All evening Elizabeth thought about the girl with the dark eyes. She puzzled about the new thatch, the mended walls, the growing garden, and the girl's old-fashioned clothes. She pictured her again standing in the cottage doorway. Who was she, and what was she doing there?

Could she be a ghost child who had come back to haunt the cottage where she had once lived and the woods where she had played. But whoever heard of a ghost feeding chickens—or ghost chickens, for that matter! Anyway, Elizabeth couldn't believe in a ghost with dimples and untidy hair.

There was another answer that was just on the edge of Elizabeth's understanding. Somehow she and the child had met across the barrier of time. She'd find the girl again, and this time they'd talk together. Elizabeth just had to see her again, and she knew that the girl was waiting for her to come.

The next morning Elizabeth woke early with a pleasant feeling of anticipation. It was Saturday, the sun was shining, and she had the whole weekend before her. She dressed quickly, pulling on jeans and a sweater—no hateful school clothes today.

Her mother was already preparing breakfast when Elizabeth came downstairs.

"You're up early." Her mother greeted her. "We've been making plans for the weekend. How would you like to go to Studland Beach today?"

"I don't mind if we don't go anywhere special," answered Elizabeth. "I can find things to do around here."

"Oh, no!" answered her mother. "We should take advantage of the weekends and do some sight-seeing, especially when the weather is good. Dad and I thought we could all go to the beach today. There's a lovely stretch of sand at Studland."

Her parents were obviously anxious to make up for yesterday's cancelled outing and had no way of knowing that it didn't matter any more.

"Doesn't Dad have to work?" asked Elizabeth.

"He can't work all the time," said her mother. "He likes a day off, too, you know."

Elizabeth dared not protest too much, so she found herself helping make sandwiches for the picnic. Then there were beach towels and swimming things and the camera to carry out to the car. At last they were ready to go.

Although it was September, the sun shone with summer warmth. The beach was so crowded that each family marked its own territory by spreading out a blanket or putting up a little canvas windbreak.

Elizabeth wandered along the wet sand close to the sea, looking for shells. Along the high water line the seaweed writhed and sloshed under a froth of yellow foam. Instead of shells, colored plastic spoons and scraps of silver paper glinted on the sand. The last high tide was marked by a line of plastic cups, smeared with black oil.

She threaded her way along the crowded beach, hearing snatches of conversation and bursts of song from transistor radios. She envied a group of teen-age girls their really neat swim suits. She was wearing her own red one-piece under her shorts. Her mother had bought it on sale at the end of last summer, and to Elizabeth it looked like something left over at the end of the season.

Elizabeth watched some children splashing in the waves. She stripped off her shorts and waded into the water. Beyond the seaweed and the froth the water was clear and, after the first shock, not too cold. Elizabeth preferred the floor of the tile swimming pool at home to the crawly feel of the sand under her toes, but the waves were exciting. Soon she found herself included in a rough, splashy game with a beach ball, and she was sorry when the game was over.

It was late afternoon when they packed up their picnic, but even then her parents weren't ready to go home.

"Let's stop at Corfe Castle," suggested her father.

Corfe Castle was a wonderful ruin. The castle stood tall and stark above the small village that sheltered at its base. High in the walls, empty doorways and windows and passages were accessible only to the birds. Within Elizabeth's reach there were small chambers to explore and walls to scramble over.

Elizabeth had visited other castles with neatly mowed lawns and excavated foundations. Little metal signs told you what once had been and where you could not go—like on the grass. Doors to crumbling spiral staircases were locked and dungeons were out of bounds. But here you could climb on the walls and peer out of narrow windows down the sheer cliff to the ribbon of highway below. Tangles of blackberries and clumps of nettles formed the only barriers.

Elizabeth loved it. Her mother did not.

"Elizabeth, do be careful!"

"Where is she now?"

"Elizabeth, stay with us!"

For once her parents were a great deal more concerned about the present than the ancient past as they followed Elizabeth through the ruins.

After exploring the castle, they went down into

the village. Behind a gift shop was a model of the castle and village as they had been long ago. The castle stood, proudly intact, behind a solid wall and heavy gates.

Looking at the model, Elizabeth asked, "Do you think the castle could be in ruins one day and then restored like this?"

"This is just how they imagine the castle was," answered her father. "They can tell a lot from foundations and even old records."

"But could the real castle, up there, ever be whole again?"

"You mean, could people rebuild it? I don't see that anyone could afford to rebuild a castle these days. The Parliamentary Engineers did a thorough job of destroying it in 1645."

"Well," said Elizabeth, a little irritated by these references to dates and things she didn't know about. Her father was always ready to tell her more than she needed to know. "I was thinking about a place that was a ruin one day and then whole the next day."

"Whole one day, and a ruin the next," said her father. "But not the other way around, I'm afraid."

So the problem of the restored cottages was something she couldn't talk about with her parents, she could see that. Not even with parents who were keen on things belonging to the past.

Here it was, time to go home. The whole day was gone, and she didn't know any more about the cottages in the woods. She'd find out tomorrow.

But the next day was the same as the day before. Her parents had everything planned.

"How would you like to go to Longleat, today?" Elizabeth's father asked her at breakfast.

"The place with the lions in the park?" asked Elizabeth, in surprise.

Longleat was a big, stately house that had opened its doors to tourists. They had to pay, of course. There they could see fine paintings and a great library and historical relics. The house belonged to the Marquis of Bath, and he knew that there were people, like Elizabeth's parents, who enjoyed seeing such things. He also knew that there were even more people, like Elizabeth, who enjoyed zoos and fun fairs and afternoon tea.

So he brought the lions to Longleat.

Ever since Elizabeth had seen the first bumper sticker advertising "The Lions of Longleat," she had wanted to go there. Her parents had always answered with a lukewarm, "Maybe, some day." And here they were suggesting it themselves.

Elizabeth's adventure at the ruined cottage was fading. Although she still wanted to see the girl again, some of the urgency was lost. She'd go tomorrow. So she didn't need to pretend to be pleased at the prospect of a visit to Longleat. She could hardly wait to be on her way.

Driving through a park where lions roamed free was very exciting. But, after seeing the lions, Elizabeth surprised her parents by choosing to go into the house rather than visit the amusement park.

The best part of the house was the kitchens. There were huge stoves and a great array of brass pots and pans. There were even life-size wax models of cooks and kitchen maids.

"How long ago was this supposed to be?" asked Elizabeth.

"Early nineteenth century, I'd guess," answered her father.

"I wonder what it was like living then?"

"Well," said Mr. Fenner. "It would depend on who you were. The people who lived in big houses like this had a good life."

"Yes, if they owned the house," said Elizabeth.

"Not just the owners," answered her father. "Many of the servants had a good life, too. They were better off than the poor in the cities, and the farm laborers. Do you know that children your age worked long days in factories and on the land?"

"Didn't they have to go to school?" asked Elizabeth.

"It wasn't until 1871 that all children here had to go to school."

"I got here just over a hundred years too late," sighed Elizabeth.

"Come off it," said her father, with a laugh. "School isn't as bad as that!"

"What did girls like me wear then?" Elizabeth asked.

"They wore long dresses and capes and bonnets and muffs. You're better off today in your jeans and shirts."

"Maybe, but not in my school uniform," said Elizabeth. "What did poor children wear?"

"They wore long dresses, too. Often the castoffs of the rich, I suppose."

Elizabeth thought about the cottage girl and her long, ragged dress. She was sure the child had been wearing the clothes of long ago. Elizabeth found she was paying more attention than she usually did to all this talk about "things past." There were some things that it might just be useful to know.

❧ 5 ❧
Ann

On Monday as soon as school was over, Elizabeth ran home and tossed her books on the window-sill. Her mother was at the dining room table with her own books and papers spread everywhere. This was a good sign. If her mother was writing, then Elizabeth could usually go her own way.

"I think I'll go for a walk," said Elizabeth, quite casually.

"Would you like me to come along?" asked her mother. "It might do me good to get out for a bit."

"That's all right, Mom. I was just going to wander about."

"Take an apple, dear," said her mother, already leafing through her papers again.

Elizabeth set off down the lane. She was excited and frightened at the same time. Suppose there was nothing to see. Suppose she had waited too long to go back and find the girl. There might be nothing in the woods but two decaying cottages inhabited by a few scampering mice. So she walked slowly to delay the time of disappointment. She kept her eyes on the path and when she reached the clearing, she was afraid to look.

The sound of children's voices made her raise her head. The beehives were there! The walls were whole and the thatch was new.

Elizabeth edged around the clearing so that she had a view of the front of the houses. There she was! She was spinning a hoop with a short stick. It bumped and wobbled on the stony path and a little ragged boy clamored for his turn.

"Give it me, Ann! Give it here!" he shouted.

The hoop clattered onto the path, and the girl gave him the stick.

Just then a shout came from inside the cottage.

"Ann! Thomas! It's supper time. Come away in."

Thomas ran in, but Ann stayed behind. She turned and looked at Elizabeth just as she had before. Her big dark eyes were kind, and a quick smile brightened her piquant little face.

A gentle look and a smile, and that was all. She turned and walked toward the cottage, leaving Elizabeth standing in the shadow of the great elm tree.

The strange girl was going to get away again! She wasn't going to stay and talk and be her friend. Elizabeth had to stop her. She couldn't lose her again.

"Wait! Wait!" shouted Elizabeth in a shrill voice. But the girl walked toward the cottage.

"Wait!" said Elizabeth, and started to run after her. She caught her at the cottage door.

Elizabeth could never understand what happened at the moment when she reached the girl, although it was to happen again and again. She reached out and touched the child—and they became one person. Elizabeth disappeared and only Ann walked in through the door, but Elizabeth was still there, thinking and looking and feeling as Ann did.

Elizabeth looked down at her feet, and they were bare and thin and brown. Her dress was faded and the hem hung crooked. On the wall was a small blotchy mirror, and Elizabeth peered into it, knowing that it would reflect back those big dark eyes under the unruly hair.

"Come and sit down, will you Ann? What do you expect to see looking out of the mirror at you? A fairy princess?"

The children around the table laughed, and Ann quickly took her place on the bench with the little ones. Everything she did came to her easily and smoothly. She accepted the pewter bowl of boiled potatoes and cabbage and knew that there would be no meat. She broke a piece off the loaf of dark bread and gave it to little Mary beside her. She chopped up the potato in Mary's bowl and blew on it and then spooned it into Mary's little birdlike mouth. She ate her own dinner hungrily.

There were six children around the table. Willy, the oldest, was a stocky boy of eleven who sat next to his mother and ate noisily. Thomas, who was eight, sat between Willy and five-year-old Fanny and was eating from both his own bowl and Fanny's bowl. Little Fanny never had any appetite, and her thin, pale face and mousy hair showed it.

Across from Willy sat Jacob, who was six and looked enough like Fanny to be her twin. Then there was Mary, who was two years old and was sitting next to Ann. Nobody spoke, but the children scuffled and ate noisily. Thomas, again reaching for Fanny's bowl, knocked over his mug of water, and it spread in a dark stain over the board table. Ann got up and dipped him another mug of water from the bucket.

The cottage was gloomy inside. The walls had been whitewashed but were discolored with smoke and the prints of dirty little hands. The gay wallpaper wasn't to be seen. The cracked linoleum was gone too, and the children walked, barefoot, on the scrubbed flagstone floor.

The cottage door opened and their father came in. He was wearing a coarse smock, and his boots were caked with mud from the field. He sat down at the head of the table, and his wife got up heavily and spooned him his share of potatoes and cabbage. She drew off a mug of ale and set it down before him.

"They'll be digging the potatoes in the top field tomorrow. Willy and Thomas and you can help," said their father to their mother.

Their mother sighed, "Maybe Ann could go tomorrow and I'll stay here with the little ones."

"Ann can mind the children better than she can carry potatoes," said her father.

"I'll go, father. I can carry them as well as Thomas," Ann said.

After supper the children ran outside, but Ann stayed with her mother and cleared off the table and straightened the room.

"You're a good girl, Ann," said her mother, as Ann stacked the bowls on the shelf and then stirred up the fire. Her father stretched out in the big chair by the hearth, and her mother sat on the settle by the window, trying to get enough light to do a bit of mending.

Then the children came trooping in, and their mother told them to get upstairs to bed. Ann took little Mary and wiped off her dirty face with a cloth hanging by the basin and led her upstairs. At the back of her mind she registered that she was going upstairs in the cottage as she had wanted to do in some other time and place. But the thought slipped away when Mary tugged her hand. She took off the little girl's dress and pinafore, then pulled on a nightshirt, and lifted her onto the big bed. Fanny climbed in the far side, and Ann slipped in the near side next to Mary. The three girls snuggled together under the rough blankets and were soon fast asleep.

Some time in the night Mary whimpered, but Ann held her close, and the little girl went back to sleep. The three boys were asleep, too, sharing another bed.

Early in the morning Ann woke with a start and looked around the strange, dim room with the two big beds. Quietly, she slipped out and stole downstairs. There were sounds of movements and murmurings from the other room. She must be quick. It was already daylight.

She fumbled with the heavy latch of the cottage door, and even as it swung open, she heard the bang of a door upstairs. Hurry! Hurry!

Across the clearing and into the deep woods she ran, and the cold dew stung her bare feet. She ran, heedless of the flowers and the singing birds, heedless of the pattern of sunlight and shade, heedless of a frightened rabbit.

Somewhere along the path her feet became clumsy with the weight of shoes, and her long, ragged skirt no longer caught in the clutching fingers of the blackberry vines. The wood thinned out, and the clock on the church tower struck five.

She stopped running and looked down at her clothes. For once she was glad to see her school uniform. She held out her hands and wondered if she had ever really looked at her own hands before. Then she tiptoed up to the church window and caught her own dim reflection. Her brown hair hung straight to her shoulders and her bangs were square across her forehead.

Reassured, she walked home and cautiously pushed open the door.

Her mother was still sitting at the table, writing.

"Have a nice walk, dear?" her mother asked.

"What time is it?" asked Elizabeth.

"Good gracious! It's after five. Come and help me with dinner," answered her mother.

"I mean, what day is it?" asked Elizabeth.

"What *day* is it?" echoed her mother. "It's Monday, of course. You've really lost track of time!"

Elizabeth sank into a chair. It was five o'clock on Monday. An hour ago she had come home from school. Yet during that hour she had eaten supper and slept through a night. It was baffling and frightening—but one thing was sure. She had to go back.

≥ 6 ≤
Scrubber Liz

The next day Elizabeth was impatient for school to be over so that she could go back to Ann's family. However, when the time came, it was raining heavily and her mother wouldn't hear of her going for a walk.

"Why don't you just stay home and watch television," her mother suggested.

It was two more days before Elizabeth could slip away. Two days during which she thought about Ann constantly. Was Ann out there playing in the woods while she sat in school? Would she be able to find Ann again as easily as she had before? Would Ann always be there waiting?

But now she was on her way down the path again with that same feeling of excitement and anxiety, wanting to hurry, yet a little afraid. But even before she reached the clearing she heard the children's voices and knew that Ann would be there.

They were picking blackberries at the edge of the garden patch. Elizabeth stood, half-hidden by a tree and watched. Fanny's and Jacob's mouths were stained with berries. Ann seemed to be intent on filling the basket, but when little Mary whimpered because her pinafore caught in the prickles, Ann pulled the briar away and found her a safer place to stand.

It was a warm September afternoon. The younger children were getting tired of working.

"Let's go over to Springfield Lane," suggested Jacob. "There's more berries there."

Jacob ran down the path that led out to the lane and the children followed, except for Ann. She seemed to know that Elizabeth was there. She turned, with a quick, inviting smile which drew Elizabeth close, and in an instant Elizabeth was Ann, hurrying down the path with her basket of berries.

She found the other children under a beech tree gathering nuts. The outer cases of the nuts lay thick on the ground.

"Look! It's a bonnet for my finger," said Fanny, fitting the four-sectioned beech husk onto her finger. It was soft and silver-gray inside. Fanny put it carefully in her pocket. She collected pretty things like a little squirrel, and like a squirrel, could never remember where she'd put them.

"Let's go to the stream," Jacob said to Thomas,

47

and the two boys scampered off down the dusty road.

Ann followed more slowly with the little girls. She picked a few berries as she went. The stream where the boys were playing ran under a bridge under the road. Ann carefully set the basket beside the bridge and scrambled down the bank. The stream ran clear, washing the flintstone bottom so that it glinted in the sunshine.

The boys were busy in a patch of waterweed.

"Want a frog?" Jacob asked Fanny, and gave it into her waiting hands.

"Me a froggy! Me a froggy!" cried little Mary.

The children splashed and played, and it was only when the sun got low, and a chill mist settled on the fields that they realized that the day was almost gone. They ran home, but only as fast as little Mary's legs would go.

Jacob was ahead going up the last hill, and he turned back to shout, "Uncle Matthew's here! I see his pony."

"Uncle Matthew's here!" The children took up the cry.

There was rabbit stew for supper that night and bowls of blackberries. But a visit from Uncle Matthew meant more than a good supper. Uncle Matthew was the best fiddler for miles around, and he always played for them. Neighbors came in, and the house shook with noise and laughter. Long after they'd been sent up to bed the children would lie listening to the magic of the fiddle and the stamping feet and the singing voices.

Uncle Matthew kept the inn at Merston. After the table was cleared, Ann heard Uncle Matthew talking to her mother.

"I want to take Ann back with me for a while. Jenny isn't well, and we need a girl to wait on the tables and do the washing up."

"She's too young, Matthew, and I need her myself, forby," answered Ann's mother.

"Just for a week. Just long enough to let Jenny get off her feet," pleaded Uncle Matthew. "We'll have her back here before you need her."

"All right! She can go with you. But for a week at the most."

The fiddling began, but Ann couldn't enjoy it. The thought of going to the inn at Merston filled her with panic, though she didn't quite know why. Uncle Matthew and Aunt Jenny were always kind to her. Then she felt closed in by the walls of the cottage and wanted to get away from all the singing and laughter. She slipped out the door into the darkness of the September night and ran swiftly down the path through the woods.

But there was someone ahead of her. An old,

stooped figure in long black clothes, was picking her way along the path. The woman paused to gather some toadstools. They were plentiful in the damp woods this time of the year.

"It's Old Scrubber Liz," Ann said to herself.

She knew the old woman, and in daylight, in the safety of a crowd of children, she had sometimes taunted her, calling, "Humpy Back" or "Old Scrubber." Some of the children threw stones, but Ann had never done that and didn't even like joining in the name-calling. Some said Old Scrubber Liz was a gypsy, and others said she was a witch. She lived by herself in a cottage on the edge of the village and was wise in the ways of healing. In spite of the children's taunting she came to their houses when they were sick, and sometimes they got better, and sometimes they didn't. Not everyone trusted Old Scrubber, but there was no one else to call on.

So Ann followed the old woman, not wanting to turn back, but afraid to overtake her. The trees were thinning and it was no longer quite so dark. Ann stepped carelessly and a twig snapped under her foot.

The old woman spun around, and a strange expression crossed her face—was it a look of fear?

"Who are you, girl?" she asked.

"Ann Lauden, ma'am," Ann answered politely.

"I know the Lauden children and don't tell me that any of those children have smooth brown hair and wear shoes on their feet. You're not one of them. But I know you! I know you!" The woman's voice rose to a shriek, and she came toward Ann, waving her cane.

"I've seen you in my house and I want you to keep away. You may mean no harm, but I don't like things I cannot understand. So keep away, child!"

Old Scrubber Liz was quite close to Ann when the darkness lightened, and she seemed to dissolve in the sunshine that filtered through the trees. Scrubber Liz vanished into nowhere. Elizabeth stood alone on the woodland path. A bright butterfly settled on a flower and a broken toadstool lay at her feet.

Elizabeth walked home feeling uneasy. She loved being with Ann and the children—or being Ann with the children. Even Ann's mother didn't guess that Elizabeth was there. But this old woman knew. Elizabeth was sure of that. Then, there were the things that she'd said that Elizabeth couldn't understand. There was the warning to keep away from her house. That made no sense.

Elizabeth would go back. She knew that. But she'd have to keep out of the way of Scrubber Liz.

The next time Elizabeth went to the cottages there was no one in sight. She stood at the edge of the clearing, as she had done the first time, and watched the cottage door. The door opened slowly and Elizabeth ran forward, expecting it to be Ann. But it was not. It was Old Scrubber Liz, who stepped out into the sunshine.

Elizabeth stopped. At first she felt more angry than frightened, standing there in the middle of the garden wearing her stupid school clothes and heavy oxford shoes. Of course, she didn't belong, and it was no wonder that the old witch-woman yelled at her and ran toward her shaking her cane.

But Scrubber Liz really meant to hit her, so Elizabeth turned and dived into the woods like a frightened rabbit running for cover. Her skirt caught on a briar, and she tugged free. The old woman was still after her, but inside the wood there was less undergrowth, and Elizabeth, dodging among the trees, soon outdistanced Scrubber Liz.

Elizabeth stopped, and the only sound she could hear was her own panting breath. She'd have to find her way back to the path to Random, without going back to the cottages, if she could. She'd quite given up any idea of finding Ann today.

It was hard to know which way to go. She was afraid to leave the cover of the woods, and she wasn't sure she'd know the path home if she found it. It never seemed to be quite the same.

It was then that she heard voices laughing and singing. A clear, high voice sang:

Here we go gathering nuts in May,
Nuts in May, nuts in May.
Here we go gathering nuts in May
On a cold and frosty morning.

Other voices joined in, and Elizabeth walked cautiously toward the singers. It was Ann and her mother and the children. They were gathering hazelnuts, and Elizabeth stood in the shadows and watched them.

Elizabeth had only seen Ann's mother inside the cottage where she had seemed colorless and tired and old. Today, Elizabeth saw that she really wasn't so very old. Maybe it was caring for six children and never getting quite enough to eat that drew the worry lines on her face and made her voice sharp and angry. Now she was in a holiday mood and let the children wrestle and play.

"Thomas, you carry the sack of nuts. We must get home now," she said.

The children ran ahead of their mother, all but Ann. She lingered behind and beckoned to Elizabeth as if she'd known that she was waiting. Elizabeth walked toward Ann—she had no choice. Ann touched her lightly and, once again, Elizabeth was Ann with all Ann's thoughts and feelings.

Ann followed her mother and the children back to the cottage. When she got there, her mother was examining a new broom that was standing beside the door.

"Scrubber Liz has been here," she said. "I wish I hadn't been gone when she came."

"I'm glad we were," said Ann.

"You'd best not talk like that about her. I'll have none of you calling names at that old woman," answered her mother. "You, most of all, Ann. She has warned me of a danger near you, but I couldn't understand her talk."

Ann turned away from her mother and busied herself stirring up the fire to boil the potatoes for supper. It frightened her to think of the old woman, though she wasn't quite sure why. It wasn't threats of danger to herself that worried her. It was more the feeling that Scrubber Liz knew things about her that she could not understand herself.

Fanny and Jacob were fighting under the table, and the small room was so full of noise and confusion that Ann could no longer think her own thoughts. Angrily, she banged down the lid on the kettle and went over to the two squabbling children. She dragged Jacob out from under the table and pushed him out the door. Fanny stayed hidden, but her whining was as annoying as Jacob's lusty yelling.

After supper the children went to bed, Ann with them. Sometime in the night a shaft of moonlight slid into the narrow window and wakened Ann. She looked at the sleeping children and then slid out of bed and tiptoed down the stairs.

She crossed the clearing noiselessly, but when she reached the path she ran fast, careless of the snapping twigs. She had reached the place where, the time before, she had seen Old Scrubber Liz, when a figure jumped out of the trees and threw her down on the path.

Ann was too frightened to struggle, and her face was pressed to the ground so that she could not scream.

"Quiet, Ann," a voice said in her ear. "Do you want to bring the gamekeeper after us?"

It was only Willy!

"What are you doing here?" she asked him.

"It's me that should be asking you," said Willy. "How can you expect to have rabbit meat for supper if you come galloping through the woods scaring all the wild creatures and calling to the gamekeeper that there's poachers in the woods?"

"But it's not right," said Ann. "Poaching, I mean."

"Starving's not right, either," said Willy. "Where are you going if you didn't come to help me?"

Ann didn't answer.

"Come on, then," said Willy. "If you can be quiet I might be able to show you something."

The two children walked noiselessly through the

woods. Willy dropped to his knees and crawled through a hedge which brought him to the edge of a field. He beckoned to Ann to squeeze up beside him, his face alive and excited. Ann drew close. Then she, too, could see what Willy saw.

Out beyond the shadow of the hedge the meadow was bathed in moonlight, and there, not ten feet from them, a family of young weasels played as if bewitched by a moonbeam. Their long, agile bodies twisted and turned as they danced and leapfrogged over one another. Sometimes one would run from the tumbling fight and execute a mad solo figure of eight and then leap back upon the others. The game was so fast and furious and one of the leaps so quick and high that Ann, crouched in the hedgerow, clapped her hands. Her clap was the midnight chime, and the magic ended. Five long, slender creatures ran for cover, and the stage was empty.

"Come on," said Willy.

There was still the work of the night to do.

Willy had set his snares in a hedgerow run. The first was undisturbed, but in the second they found a hare. Ann would have let the gentle creature go, but such a thought never passed through Willy's mind. He killed it, quick and neat, and together they made for home.

They were almost back to the cottage when they heard the keeper.

"We'll be all right if he hasn't his dog," said Willy.

They stood together in the wood and waited. The keeper passed quite close but, like them, he was intent on getting home.

"Go on, Willy—I'll follow," said Ann.

When they reached the path, she headed away from the cottages toward the church and the lane to Random Cottage.

Somewhere along the way daylight flooded the sky, and Elizabeth ran confidently home from her walk.

"Where did you go today?" asked her mother.

"Oh, nowhere," answered Elizabeth casually, and then couldn't help adding, "I saw some weasels."

"Weasels—those nasty slinky creatures?" asked her mother.

"They're not nasty. They're beautiful! They were dancing in the moonlight."

"Moonlight at five o'clock," said her mother, and shook her head. "I used to think you'd no imagination, but you do dream up the strangest things!"

Elizabeth wanted to say more about the madcap weasels, but she couldn't. She'd have to wait and talk about it with Willy. It was their secret.

≈ 7 ≈
Michael

The next afternoon it was raining. Elizabeth came home and found her mother cleaning out the garage.

"Elizabeth, could you help me sort out these bottles and jars? I'm hoping to make enough room in here for our suitcases. We've been falling over them in the bedroom ever since we came, and I'm sure we could fit them in here."

There had never been any question of putting the car in the garage. It was much too full of broken chairs, wobbly lamps, ornaments, bits of vacuum cleaners, radios, and an old television set.

"We could have a garage sale with all this stuff," said Elizabeth, looking around.

"I doubt if any of this has any value," said her mother. "Obviously nobody ever throws anything away—or mends it either."

"What shall I do with the jars?" asked Elizabeth,

shaking a family of sowbugs out of one of them.

"Arrange them on that shelf. Though why they are all being kept, I don't know. Still, it's not up to us to throw out the landlord's possessions."

"Look at this," said Elizabeth, holding up an old stone jar to show her mother.

"Better not break that one," answered her mother. "I bet it's a hundred years old. That's a real antique. We'll let Dad see it. Maybe everything here isn't worthless."

"Can I have it?" asked Elizabeth.

An idea was taking shape.

"I don't think you can," said her mother, slowly. "It might be valuable. Why would you want it?"

"Well . . . it's old, and I think it's interesting."

Mrs. Fenner looked a little puzzled. It wasn't the sort of answer she expected from Elizabeth, who was impatient with anything older than last week. It would be nice, she thought, if Elizabeth would learn a little appreciation for the past. So she answered, "I suppose you can take it up to your room. We'll ask Dad about it."

Elizabeth ran off before her mother could change her mind. The jar was important because it was going to be a present for Ann. First she washed it thoroughly. Then she counted out the money in her purse and ran down to the village shop.

"A jar of jam, please," said Elizabeth.

"Strawberry, raspberry, peach, plum?" asked the shop girl.

Elizabeth looked at the display of jam.

"Blackberry," she answered.

It had to be a kind you might find in a kitchen long ago, and Elizabeth knew they ate blackberries. She wasn't sure about the others, especially peaches.

Back home, in the privacy of her own bedroom, she transferred the jam from its glass container to the stone jar. It was a sticky business, but she could hear her mother moving about downstairs, so she didn't want to risk going to the bathroom or kitchen to wash. Instead she licked her fingers.

It was good jam, she thought. Just the right sort of thing to take. She couldn't put a jar of Robinson's Blackberry Jam on the shelf in the cottage, but she could put this stone jar beside the jars that were already there.

She'd sometimes felt sad when she came back from Ann's life and compared how much she had with what they had. Maybe there was some way she could help them. Maybe that was why she had found her way into their lives. The little kids didn't mind having nothing, but the parents and Willy and even Ann worked awfully hard to provide bread with no jam and potatoes with no meat.

Meantime, Mrs. Fenner continued to feel pleased that Elizabeth had been interested in the old jar. If she had realized how far Elizabeth's interest in the past was taking her, she would have been more worried than pleased. But Mrs. Fenner was working on a story these days and also was busy with shopping and cooking and washing—all of which took much more time here than back in Timberhill. So she didn't realize that Elizabeth was absorbed in an adventure that was pulling her back into the past, pulling more strongly each day.

Elizabeth hurried home from school the next day and smuggled the jar of jam out of the house.

When she reached the edge of the clearing, there was no one about. She stood waiting. She saw a door open finally, not to Ann's cottage, but to the cottage next door. Fanny and Jacob came running out.

"Now, you're not to be going home," a voice called after them.

The two children ran across the grass and took the path that led to Springfield Lane. Quietness settled over the clearing again.

Elizabeth waited for a long time and then tiptoed toward the house. If she couldn't find Ann today, she'd leave the jar of jam and go home.

She pushed open the cottage door and stepped inside. The room was dim and hot and steamy. The fire was built up high although it was a mild afternoon, and two kettles hung steaming over the flames.

Upstairs a door slammed, and slow shuffling steps sounded on the stairs. The stairs led down into the other room, and in a minute, whoever was coming would be in the doorway in line with Elizabeth. She quickly ducked behind the high-backed settle. There she waited, holding her breath, and then peered out anxiously. She drew back quickly, and her heart pounded so loudly that she was sure it would give her away.

It was Old Scrubber Liz.

The old woman shuffled to the fireplace, looking more like a witch than ever, and lifted a steaming pot from the fire. She shook some dried leaves into it, muttering to herself as she did so.

She stayed by the fire for what seemed a very long time to Elizabeth and then, at last, poured two mugs of tea from the kettle. Was it only tea, Elizabeth wondered, or was it some magic brew?

Suddenly a cry came from the upstairs room. Elizabeth nearly dropped the jam jar in her fright, but the old woman just took up the mugs and shuffled back toward the stairs. As soon as she was gone, Elizabeth slipped out the door and ran toward the path that led back home. She didn't even take time to cross the room and put the jar on the shelf but took it with her.

She had just started down the path when she came

face to face with Ann. Ann looked pinched and white, but she broke into a sudden smile on seeing Elizabeth.

"I was lookin' for you," she said.

It was the first time Ann had ever spoken directly to her, and Elizabeth felt a thrill of delight. Maybe now, through words, they could understand this strange experience.

But Ann ran to her with outstretched arms—and then Elizabeth was Ann. Elizabeth was Ann and understood what was happening back at the cottage. There was going to be a new baby. Her mother's weariness and her slow, heavy walk had been because of the baby.

A few hours ago she had been sent off to find Scrubber Liz.

"Run, child!" her mother had said, in a voice edged with fear. She had been standing, holding the edge of the table so tight that her knuckles were white on her cracked, brown hands.

"It'll be nice havin' a baby to hold again," Ann had said, but her mother didn't seem to hear. She just gave a little sob that sent Ann scuttling off to find Old Liz.

Scrubber Liz was already on her way to the cottage when Ann met her. The old woman told the children to stay away from the house, and none of them needed to be told a second time.

Ann had wandered restlessly around the clearing and then had set off down the path through the woods again. She had felt lonely and frightened and finally had turned back to look for Fanny and Jacob. Even being with the little ones would be better than feeling so alone.

But close to the cottage, on meeting Elizabeth, her courage had returned, and no longer interested in finding Fanny and Jacob, she had pushed her way into the dim kitchen. The house was quiet. Then, from upstairs, came a thin, new-born baby cry. Ann didn't hesitate but clattered up the bare, wooden stair and burst into the bedroom.

Old Scrubber Liz scowled at her. "You bairns were told to stay out of here today. But since you're here, take this wee bundle and sit by the fire and keep him warm."

Ann turned first to her mother.

"Oh, Mother!"

Her mother looked up at Ann and gave that quick little smile that often lit up Ann's own face.

"He's little Michael. Take care of him, Ann."

Ann took the baby in her arms. He was little and red and wizened. His eyes were puffy and closed. He pressed a tiny closed fist against his chin. Trembling, Ann carried him downstairs and sat near the hot fire. She sang softly to him, rocking back and forth on the chair.

The door opened. Ann's father stood there, filling the doorway and blocking off the light. He looked at Ann and the baby and then said, jerking his head upward, "Is she all right?"

"Yes," answered Ann.

"What is it?" he asked, coming over to the baby.

"It's a boy," answered Ann.

Ann's father looked glumly at the babe and then said, "Better a boy than a girl, but it will still need to be fed."

Then he shook his head and walked over to the stairs.

Ann sat and looked at the tiny baby, and she felt sad. Though she could not have found words to express it and scarcely understood the thought, she was feeling that here in her arms was the whole miracle of creation. Yet to her father it was only another hungry mouth to feed where there were already too many. Better a boy than a girl, he had said. A boy would someday work in the fields. But didn't she do her share in the fields and help in the house, forby?

She cradled the baby in her arms. It shouldn't be like this. Everyone should start off wanted and loved.

Before long the children came home for supper, and Ann gave them bread and potatoes.

Then their father said to Willy, "Get out the Book, Willy."

Willy went through to the other room and lifted

the big family Bible down from its place on the oak dresser. Then he got a quill pen and ink. Opening the Bible to the second page, he wrote in large, careful, wobbly letters:

MICHAEL JOHN LAUDEN
19 SEPTEMBER 1871

Ann watched. She looked at the long list of names in the front of the Bible, and she knew which name was hers. And that was all she knew. Ann just ached with longing to read all these words, but she'd never get the chance. Even her father couldn't read. Willy was the only one. He had gone to the Dame School in the village and had learned to read a little and to write a little, but he hadn't liked going to school. Willy wasn't one for sitting still.

Ann had once followed Willy to school and peered in the doors and windows. The children sat at wooden desks, and there was a switch in the corner to punish those who didn't learn their lessons. Ann thought she might learn by listening at the door, for she was much too shy to go inside. Besides, her father saw no reason for a girl to have book learning.

However, the teacher had slammed the door shut, so Ann had crouched in the doorway, warmed by the sun, and had listened to the drone of the children's voices as they recited their tables. She must have fallen asleep because the door burst open and children tumbled out over her. Some of the children called her names and laughed at her ragged dress, so she retreated to the woods.

She never tried to go to school again.

The Dame School was closed now, and a big new school was being built in the village. The government had said that there was to be a school in every village and town and that every child had to go. No matter what the government said, she wouldn't learn to read and write. She was too old to go to school. She was ten years old and would be working soon.

Ann sat by the fire, holding Michael tight. Little Michael would go to school. Maybe even Mary and Fanny and Jacob, too. But how Ann wished she could read a book. It just wasn't fair, it wasn't fair. . . .

The baby became more and more Ann's complete charge. When he whined and fretted, she never tired of holding him. His mother nursed him and laid him in the little cradle where each child had slept in turn. But Ann lifted him out when he whimpered and held him close.

Sometimes, in the early morning, when Ann first woke there were thoughts of another life—was it her real life?—but always, the baby's thin cry held her.

Little Michael cried a lot, and it was always a thin, tired cry. Often he spat up his milk.

"I wish you'd go and ask Scrubber Liz to come

back and see the baby," Ann's mother said to her. "Go now, while the little ones are out playing."

It was a damp, gray day, and Ann pulled her brown wool shawl around her shoulders. She followed the path through the wood to Lower Waterberry. She was almost at the village church when she found that she was no longer ragged, barefoot Ann, but Elizabeth again. She realized it had to happen—she had followed the path home.

But what about Michael? Would Ann find Scrubber Liz?

Then, Elizabeth wondered, what about herself? Would she reach home and find that only an hour or so had passed, when she had been gone for over two weeks? The church clock was, as always, striking five. The lane was empty, but that was usual, too.

Outside the door of Random Cottage she stood for a minute, afraid to go in. Slowly, she pushed the door open and waited in the doorway. Her mother looked up casually from the evening newspaper.

"That you, dear? Nice walk?"

Elizabeth walked into the room.

"Why, how pale you are!" said her mother, suddenly concerned. "You're getting more peaky and quiet every day, Elizabeth. Where do you go on these walks of yours?"

Her mother fussed around, but Elizabeth felt only

relief. She was back where she belonged. She listened to her mother's questions and tried to give offhand answers, but she was tired—too tired to talk. It was as if, by crowding weeks of living into an hour, she had exhausted herself.

"I wish you had some friends here, Elizabeth. Back in Timberhill there were always girls coming and going. Haven't you made any friends here?"

"I have a friend," said Elizabeth slowly.

"Is it that nice little girl, Nancy? Let's ask her to tea tomorrow. Maybe we could take her somewhere on Saturday."

"I can't ask her to tea," Elizabeth answered, and felt a fleeting sadness that her mother could never know Ann.

"*Can't* ask her to tea! What nonsense!" said Mrs. Fenner impatiently. "I'll phone her mother and arrange it now."

"Please don't, Mom. I'll ask Nancy myself sometime. But not yet. Please not now."

❧ 8 ❧
New Friends

The next morning when Elizabeth awakened in her own small bed, she missed little Mary's snuggling warmth, and she even missed Michael's fretful morning cry. Was Ann sitting rocking him by the fire, listening to the sounds of the cottage— her mother getting the breakfast, the rhythmic thump of the cradle, and the voices of the children as they crowded to the table waiting for their bowls of porridge to be filled?

Elizabeth then noticed that her own house was unusually quiet. She dressed quickly and went downstairs. Her mother was sitting at the table, frowning over a shopping list.

"Here you are at last," said her mother. "I'll get you some breakfast."

"Have you had yours? Where's Dad?" asked Elizabeth, looking around at the tidy room. It didn't have an "early morning" look, and the hands of the big grandfather clock pointed to ten-thirty.

"Is it really ten-thirty?" asked Elizabeth, following her mother to the kitchen. "School! I'm missing school! Where's my lunch? I'll have to run."

"It's all right, Elizabeth," said her mother, going through to the kitchen. "School can wait! You've been so quiet and tired lately that I didn't even try to wake you this morning. Perhaps school is too much for you here."

"Oh, no, Mother! School's all right now. I hardly notice it."

That, at least, was true.

Elizabeth was suddenly anxious not to have anything change. If she stopped going to Waterberry School, then there might be no reason for them to live in Waterberry. Her father would want to be closer to a big library. She must make her mother see that everything was fine at school.

"You're so quiet and have so few friends here," her mother said.

Elizabeth glumly munched her way through a bowl of cornflakes. What would she say to Mr. Ranton when she walked into school at 11 o'clock? She could hardly say she'd been too tired to come to school. It might be easier not to go at all today— but then she had to convince her mother that she liked school here. Bother them all!

"What'll I say to Mr. Ranton?" she asked her mother.

"I'll write him a note explaining that I think

you've been finding school rather a strain. It's been a big change for you," said Mrs. Fenner soothingly.

Elizabeth sighed. You couldn't take a note like that to Rant-'n-Rave. Maybe it was because her mother wrote novels, but it seemed to Elizabeth that her mother always wrote too much to teachers. Other kids took notes that said, "Please excuse Mary Jane's absence from school." But Elizabeth's notes gave her whole medical history. Once her absence note had even gone on to the second page. And her father's excuse notes were worse—he tried to be funny. So she'd have to get by without a note.

"I'll take an apple for lunch," said Elizabeth. "And I don't suppose I need a note. I'll just explain."

Elizabeth walked slowly down the hill to school. She hoped it would be playtime and that she could merge with the crowds of children, but when she turned the corner she saw that the playground was deserted. She unbolted the gate, and it clanged shut behind her. She felt that curious eyes must be staring from every window, watching the girl who came two hours late to school.

She stood outside her classroom door gathering her courage. She couldn't hear a sound from inside. It was as if everyone was holding his breath waiting for her to enter. She really was afraid of old Rant-'n-Rave when he shouted. He'd never shouted at her, but until now she'd never given him reason. Two hours late for school seemed reason enough.

She pushed open the door. Every head was bent over an arithmetic problem, but every head raised, hoping that whoever was coming through the door was about to deliver them from arithmetic.

Elizabeth walked over to Mr. Ranton's table and said in a quiet voice, "I'm very sorry I'm late."

"That's all right," said Mr. Ranton. "The blue arithmetic book, page 64, the first five problems."

Elizabeth walked to her seat, and even smiled to Mandy as she passed the front row of seats. Mr. Ranton must have figured that she had a really good reason for being late. After all, you might be fifteen minutes late because you'd overslept, but nobody ever slept in two hours on a school day. Even the blue arithmetic book didn't seem so awful today.

After school Nancy waited for Elizabeth at the gate.

"Do you want to come down to the post office and buy sweets?" Nancy asked.

"I don't have any money with me," answered Elizabeth.

"I've got five pence, and I'll share with you," said Nancy.

So the two girls walked down to the village. Outside the post office was a huge baby carriage, or pram. There was nothing unusual in that. There were often prams left outside the shops while the mothers were inside shopping.

What made Elizabeth notice the pram was the thin, fretful cry from the baby inside. It sounded just like Michael. Elizabeth peered under the hood of the pram. Tiny fists were waving, and all she could see of the baby was a red face and a huge, wide mouth. The baby had been twisting and turning so that his bonnet half-covered his face, and the satin bow was tight under his chin.

Elizabeth leaned into the pram and rearranged the baby's hat and talked gently. The baby's shrill cry stopped, and Elizabeth gently rocked the pram.

"Come on!" said Nancy.

"You choose the sweets," answered Elizabeth. "I'll stay and keep the baby quiet."

Nancy shrugged and went into the shop. It was crowded at this time of day when school got out. Children went in to buy sweets and comics, and mothers stopped in to pick up groceries they had forgotten earlier. The post office was more than a place to mail letters.

Elizabeth stood rocking the pram and talking to the baby. He looked older than Michael and was much rounder and rosier. She admired his clean, soft white clothes and his lacy pillow. How she wished Michael could have a bonnet like that!

Maybe she could take him one. Then she remembered the jam. What had happened to it? She remembered she'd had it when she had met Ann on the path, but where had it gone after that? She didn't know. Maybe that proved it was no use trying to take presents into the past.

She looked again at the baby in his fresh new clothes. She loved his bonnet with its lacy brim and satin ribbon. If only she could give Michael something pretty instead of the matted wool shawl he wore. She wondered if, as Ann, she could give him something—but then Ann never had any money.

Just then a tall young lady hurried out of the shop with an assortment of parcels.

"Hello," she said to Elizabeth. "I wondered why he'd stopped crying. He does like to be bounced."

The young mother looked at Elizabeth in a friendly way. "Want to push him?" she asked.

"Oh, yes!" said Elizabeth, and carefully released the pram brake with her foot.

Just then Nancy came out of the post office and ran to join them.

"This is my friend Nancy," said Elizabeth, and added to Nancy, "She's letting me push her baby."

"I thought we'd go to my house," said Nancy. Clearly pushing a baby carriage was not the way Nancy would choose to spend the afternoon.

"Yes, you go on with your friend," urged the young mother.

Elizabeth hesitated, but Nancy decided the matter

by saying, "Push the baby! You can come to my house some other time." And she stalked off without offering Elizabeth any sweets.

So Elizabeth pushed the pram up the street and listened to the mother talk. She was Mrs. Wilson, but told Elizabeth to call her Patsy. The baby was called Kevin.

When they reached the Wilson's house—one of the little boxlike houses at the edge of the village— they levered the pram up the three front steps and parked it in the narrow hallway. Then Patsy, carrying Kevin, led Elizabeth into the little sitting room, which was cluttered with furniture for Kevin. There was a high chair, a playpen, a bath, a screen draped with baby clothes, a ball, and an assortment of toys.

Patsy flicked on the switch of an electric heater with her foot.

"Would you take Kevin?" she said to Elizabeth. "I'll go and make tea and heat his bottle. Usually he's crying so much that I don't have time to make tea or put away the shopping before I feed him."

Elizabeth sat in a rather stiff, upright chair and held Kevin. He looked up at her and gave her a wavery, toothless smile and drooled a little. Elizabeth sat him up a little straighter, and he smiled again.

Patsy came in carrying a tray and looked around for somewhere to set it down. She balanced it across the corner of the playpen.

"Donald says he doesn't see why we have to have this room so full of baby things, but I say we'll just have to get used to it. I wish, though, that we had a bigger place."

Elizabeth agreed that they needed more room or fewer things. She didn't say anything.

Patsy took Kevin and laid him in the playpen. Then she handed Elizabeth a cup of tea.

"How come you know so much about babies?" asked Patsy. "Do you have a baby at your house?"

"No," said Elizabeth. "I just like them."

She would have liked to talk to Patsy about little Michael, how pale and fretful he was, but there was just no way of explaining *who* he was, so it was better not to start. Besides, she'd better go home. Time wouldn't be standing still today, and her mother might worry if she were late.

"I'd better go home now," said Elizabeth.

"Can you come again?" asked Patsy.

"Why, sure!" answered Elizabeth.

Elizabeth met her mother on the lane to Random Cottage.

"I was coming to get you," said Mrs. Fenner.

"To get me?" repeated Elizabeth.

"Were you kept in for being late this morning?" asked her mother.

"Oh, no!" said Elizabeth. "I've been visiting a friend."

"Oh, dear!" said Mrs. Fenner, attempting to laugh. "I was so sure that awful Rant-'n-Rave had kept you in for being late that I was on my way to have it out with him!"

"Mother!" said Elizabeth. "Even if he had kept me in, you couldn't do that!"

"Well, it didn't happen. Were you at Nancy's?"

"No, I wasn't at Nancy's," answered Elizabeth, feeling a little uncomfortable at the way she had left Nancy. "I met another girl and went to her house. She has a cute little baby called Kevin."

"Her little brother?" asked Mrs. Fenner.

They had reached home, and Mrs. Fenner pushed the front door open and held it for Elizabeth.

"Kevin is her own baby," answered Elizabeth.

Mrs. Fenner stopped in the doorway.

"Her own baby?" she asked.

"She's grown up, but she's not old," said Elizabeth.

"I thought maybe you'd make friends with some girls in your class at school," sighed Mrs. Fenner.

At supper Elizabeth told her father about her new friend.

"Wouldn't you be better playing than minding a baby?" asked her mother.

"Oh, Mother, I wish *we* had a baby. Couldn't we have one? I don't see why I have to be the only child in this family."

Her parents were taken aback. They looked at each other across the supper table.

"A baby wouldn't be company for you, Elizabeth," said her mother.

"It would, and I'd do all the work. I'd get up in the night if it cried."

"There's more to it than who does the work, Elizabeth," said her father, pushing his chair back from the table. "Your mother and I believe that most of the problems in the world today are because there are too many people. Wars, violence, pollution, and all the rest. People cause these problems—too many people. We have to settle for fewer children if there is to be any future for the world at all."

"Fewer shouldn't be just one," said Elizabeth. "It's not fair to me."

"War, violence, and pollution aren't fair, either, Elizabeth. We can't do very much about them, but we're bound to do what we can. Smaller families are the first step."

"Maybe you could adopt a baby," suggested Elizabeth. "If it's already born, you wouldn't be adding anybody. You could even adopt a whole family."

Elizabeth's father got up from his chair, laughing. He ruffled her hair as he passed her.

"I'm happy with the family we've got."

Then he hid himself behind his newspaper, and Elizabeth knew that was the end of the discussion, so she went up to her bedroom. She threw herself on her bed and stared up at the cracked ceiling. It looked like a map, a road map of Britain, showing the main roads as wide cracks and the secondary roads as narrow cracks. The narrow crack above her would be the road to Patsy's house, and the very fine line was the path to Ann's cottage.

She began to compare the houses in her mind. Patsy's front room was about the same size as Ann's —and they were, neither of them, big enough. Patsy's was full of things, and Ann's was full of kids. At least you could get rid of things if you found you didn't need them.

Elizabeth fell asleep following the maze of roads on the ceiling. She turned off a main crack onto a narrow road and then followed a fine line. Each road was closed in by high, gray walls. The road got narrower and the walls got higher. Even when she turned and retraced her steps, the road closed in more and the high walls squeezed against her. At last there was nowhere to go, she couldn't get back . . . she couldn't get back . . . she couldn't get back. . . .

Elizabeth awakened, shaking with fright, and found her mother and father beside her bed.

"I couldn't get back," she sobbed. "I followed the path, and there was no way back."

"It was just a dream," her mother assured her. "We heard you shout. It was a dream. You fell asleep without even getting into your pajamas. Now get undressed, and we'll have hot chocolate downstairs before you go back to sleep."

But even hot chocolate and her parents' company didn't dispel the agony of the dream. Suppose, suppose it was a warning—a path with no way back. Maybe she shouldn't go again. But could she give up Ann and little Michael now? Or was she prepared to give up all this if there was no way back? She didn't know.

❧ 9 ❧
Potato Picking

The pattern in the playground had changed during the weeks that Elizabeth had attended Waterberry School. The girls no longer brought their skipping ropes, and even the boys had forsaken the soccer field. It was conker season.

Conkers were the hard, shiny brown nuts of the horse chestnut trees, and the children knew every chestnut tree within miles. They trailed through the yellow and brown leaves and pounced on the nuts. Sometimes the green outer case was split, and you could see the gleaming chestnut pushing to get out. Other times you had to stamp on the nut with careful force—enough to break the outside case, but not enough to smash the nut.

Elizabeth liked looking for chestnuts. There was a tree that hung over the lane, and every morning she scuffed through the leaves. She loved the sheen of the nut and the white, white inside of the outer case when it was first opened. Sometimes two, or even three, nuts grew inside a shell with flattened faces pressed close together.

Once you had your nut, you bored a hole in it with a nail and then threaded it on to a string. This was your conker. You used it to hit someone else's chestnut. Or they hit yours.

Elizabeth and Joanna Webster were standing together near the fence that ran along the back of the playground, separating it from a ploughed field. Elizabeth held out her nut, and Joanna ran her fingers down the string to steady it and then wrapped her own string around her hand and gave a quick flick.

"You jerked away! You jerked away!" shouted Joanna indignantly.

"I'm sorry," said Elizabeth. "I don't mean to. Really! Try again."

This time Elizabeth closed her eyes and forced her hand to keep still. The nuts crashed, but neither broke.

"Your turn, Elizabeth."

Elizabeth took aim quickly and missed Joanna's nut by at least three inches. The strings twisted together, and Joanna untangled them.

"Your string's too long, and you don't aim," said Joanna.

"Can I play the winner?" asked Christy.

"You can play Joanna now," said Elizabeth. "I'll watch."

It only took Christy one swing to demolish Joanna's nut.

"I'll play you now," said Christy.

"I'll give Joanna my nut, and you can play her," suggested Elizabeth. "I always get them tangled."

Elizabeth stood watching. She liked watching better than playing. Gradually she became aware of someone standing near her. She turned and then took a step back, her heart beating wildly with surprise and fear.

It was Ann.

Ann was looking hungrily at the school and the playground. She was dirtier than usual. Her clogs were caked with mud and draped over her shoulders was a brown woolen shawl. Her face was streaked with dirt.

Elizabeth wanted to run back into the school. This was now. This was schooltime. She couldn't disappear into Ann's life now. She didn't want to! She wanted to play conkers and learn spelling and . . .

But Ann turned to her and smiled and then reached out and touched Elizabeth.

The noise of the whole schoolyard of playing children receded and became still. The children grew thin and faded like shadows on a cloudy day. The playground itself became a weedy field, and even the school disappeared almost to its foundations.

Elizabeth tried to cling to the present, but she felt herself fading as she merged into Ann, so that only Ann stood there gazing at the place where they were going to build a school.

Willy came up beside her.

"I wish they would hurry and build that school," said Ann.

"What good will a school be?" asked Willy.

"I could learn to read and write," answered Ann.

"Readin' and writin' isn't so great," said Willy, secure in knowing that he could sound out words and write his name.

"I want to learn," said Ann.

"You'll never learn now," said Willy. "And how would readin' and writin' help you gather potatoes and turnips?"

Willy turned and trudged off up the field. Ann followed, though she'd rather have stood and watched the men working on the school. They were starting to lay the red brick walls.

As she stooped to pick the new potatoes out of the furrow and scrabbled in the dirt to see that she hadn't missed any, her thoughts were still on reading and writing. Willy was wrong. Even if she did have to gather potatoes and turnips, being able to read and write would make a difference. It would make a difference inside. If you could read and write then, maybe, someday, you could do other things. If you could read and write, then you could also hope.

85

Ann straightened her slight body and swung the sack onto her shoulder. It was only half-full, but half a sack was all she could carry down to the wagon.

She stumbled on a clod of earth. She'd been working since early morning, and her shoulders ached, and her back ached, and her legs ached. She was hungry, too, but she had eaten her bread and cheese an hour ago.

"Hurry along there, girl!" shouted Farmer Featherby, who was standing near the wagon. He scowled and shouted at everybody, but Ann cringed at his angry voice. The little boys aped him and made faces at him behind his back, but Ann was much too cautious for that.

It was a long day. At last dusk crept over the field, and Ann and Willy and Thomas trudged home with their father. The children slid into their places on the bench and ate their supper in silence. Little Michael cried in his cradle by the fire, but Ann was too tired to comfort him.

"Matthew was here, today," her mother said to her father. "He wants Ann back at the inn again. He'd have taken her today."

"Will he be back?" asked her father.

"He'll be back tomorrow. Shall we let her go?"

"She'd be better there than in the potato field," answered her father. So the matter was settled.

Deep inside Ann was the feeling that she didn't

want to go with Uncle Matthew to the inn at Merston. There was some reason why she should stay here in the cottage. Was it little Michael? No, there was something else to keep her here, but she was too tired to think, so she stumbled up to bed.

In the night Ann awakened to the cry of a lonely owl. She lay in the darkness and thought again of going to the inn at Merston and was suddenly afraid.

She crept out of bed, as she had done before, and ran through the dark woods. The darkness pressed down on her, and she fought back her fears. Then the darkness faded, and when she reached the church the sun was high over head and the hands of the clock pointed to a quarter to one. Elizabeth stood in the old churchyard dressed in her school clothes and thought things out.

If it was a quarter to one, then the children would still be in the playground for their lunchtime break. Elizabeth could hear them. No time had passed since she had been playing conkers with Christy and Joanna, so she must hurry back to school.

Instead of going up the lane toward home, she ran down toward the main road and the school. Just as she turned the corner, the bell rang and the children ran to line up in front of the doors. Elizabeth pushed open the gate and ran to join her line.

But she did not come in unnoticed.

"Elizabeth!"

Miss Cooper was in charge today and called Elizabeth to her.

"Elizabeth, what were you doing outside the playground?"

"I went home," said Elizabeth.

It seemed the easiest answer to give and one which might be believed.

"Were you feeling ill?" asked Miss Cooper, coming nearer. "You look dreadfully pale, child. You look as if you'd seen a ghost."

"I'm all right," said Elizabeth.

"Was your mother home?"

Elizabeth shook her head.

"Perhaps you'd better go into the teachers' room and lie down," said Miss Cooper kindly.

"I'm all right. Really!" said Elizabeth. "I'd rather go to my class."

Miss Cooper watched Elizabeth follow the other children into the school and stood for a moment with a puzzled frown. Then she shrugged and hurried to her own classroom.

Even sitting here in school, Elizabeth was worried. She had liked sliding back into Ann's life when it had been her choice, but now she felt closed in and pursued by Ann. The time might come when living two lives was too much for her, and she could be only one—Ann or Elizabeth. Which would she be?

Ann had many things Elizabeth didn't. There

were Mary and Fanny and Jacob and Thomas, and even Willy, and there were the good times they had together. The woods belonged to them far more than they belonged to Farmer Featherby; they knew them with love and had visited the secret places. And there was wee Michael who cried in his cradle but was content when Ann held him. Elizabeth felt that in a way he belonged as much to her as to Ann.

But there was the drudgery and the poverty and the cold and the hunger. And there was ignorance. Ignorance went beyond not knowing how to read and write. It meant knowing nothing outside your own life. It meant not having the doctor come when you were sick. It caused fear—an evil kind of fear.

It was surely better to be living now. Her Dad had said last night that there were problems—problems she couldn't solve. There was oil on the beaches and litter in the park. There were fears, too. Just looking at the news showed that frightening things happen. And some day the earth might run out of food and space and clean water and energy.

But still there was a chance to change things— more now than in Ann's time. You could go to school. You weren't trapped like Ann was. You had more choice . . . more hope. . . .

The secret lay in learning and understanding and knowing.

"Elizabeth!"

Old Rant-'n-Rave's angry voice broke into her thoughts.

"What was the date of the Spanish Armada?"

Elizabeth looked blankly at Mr. Ranton.

"Would it be too much trouble for you to tell us the date of the Spanish Armada?" he asked sarcastically.

Elizabeth groped in her mind for a date.

"Ten sixty-six," she suggested in a small voice. Something had happened then, but judging from the giggles around her, it hadn't involved the Spanish Armada.

"Missed by over five hundred years," shouted Rant-'n-Rave and a piece of chalk flew past Elizabeth's ear. It was lucky his aim was always wild when he was angry.

"Sometimes I think I'm wasting my time here," Mr. Ranton said.

"Oh, no, sir!" said Elizabeth. "I was just thinking that learning and understanding and knowing things are really important. That's why I missed what you said."

Mr. Ranton stood blinking at Elizabeth. Was she being impertinent? He couldn't tell. The class sat open-mouthed, hoping that Elizabeth had more to say. At that moment she changed from being the new girl to a valued member of their side.

≽ 10 ≼
Visitors

Elizabeth came home from school that day and noticed at once that the cottage was particularly clean and neat. The brasses gleamed on the sideboard and great bowls of late chrysanthemums decorated the deep window sills. A fire cast a flickering light on the white walls and the whole house had a polished look.

"Who's coming?" asked Elizabeth, hanging her coat on the peg on the back of the door.

"Is it so obvious?" said her mother with a laugh. "Grandma and Grandpa Fenner are coming tonight. Dad has gone to the station to meet them."

"I didn't even know they'd left Oregon," said Elizabeth. "I thought they were coming over for Christmas."

"They *are* coming for Christmas, but they plan to tour first. However, when they got to London, they found their car wouldn't be ready for several days, so they decided to come here by train and wait."

"I'm glad the car wasn't there. Now we don't have to wait till Christmas to see them," said Elizabeth.

"Is that Dad's car?" asked Mrs. Fenner. "That will be them!"

Elizabeth ran out and then felt suddenly shy when her grandparents climbed out of the car and shouted excited greetings.

"There she is!"

"My, how she's grown! Quite the young lady!"

"And look at those smart school clothes!"

"A tie, no less!"

"So much smarter than these jeans all the girls wear at home." That was Grandma.

"I like jeans," said Elizabeth, but was enfolded in a perfumed embrace before she could say anything more in defense of comfortable clothes.

Mrs. Fenner was an elegant lady. Today she was wearing pants herself—a well-tailored pink pantsuit that matched her pink pearls and gray-pink hair. Even after a day on a train she was still well-pressed and pale pink and perfumed. Elizabeth knew why her mother had gone to such pains to clean the cottage. Mrs. Fenner, senior, wouldn't be impressed by two hundred years of history unless there was running hot and cold water and central heating. And the cottage didn't have central heating.

Grandpa Fenner was a mild little man with a

twinkle in his eye. He didn't ever say much to Elizabeth but often slipped her a quarter for candy.

The grandparents followed Elizabeth into the house, exclaiming with delight. "Quaint" was her grandmother's favorite expression about the house, and Elizabeth began to feel that maybe "quaint" wasn't altogether good.

Elizabeth's mother surpassed herself with supper. There was steak and kidney pie and mushrooms and salad. This was followed by fruit and biscuits and cheese. Then everyone gathered around the fire in the sitting room, and there was a lot of cheerful chatter about friends back in Timberhill. Grandma and Grandpa lived quite close to Elizabeth so they knew all her friends. Monica's brother had got a new bike for his birthday, a ten-speed. Grandma thought it was ridiculous the way Monica was allowed to tear around on it.

There was a pause in the conversation. Then Grandma Fenner suddenly half rose from her chair and said, "Look!" in a hoarse voice.

All eyes turned toward the cottage door. A thick red velvet curtain hung across the doorway to help keep out the drafts that sneaked around the old, ill-fitting door.

Elizabeth could see nothing to excite her grandmother, but she stared at the door like the others. Her first thought had been that Ann had come into the cottage and that, somehow or other, she was visible to Grandma.

"Look!" shouted Grandma again.

And then Elizabeth saw it, too.

It was only a spider. Admittedly, it was one of the largest, fattest spiders Elizabeth had seen, but it didn't call for hysterics.

Elizabeth's mother walked over and quite casually scooped up the fat spider, groped behind the curtain for the door handle, opened the door, and tossed the spider out.

"I knew it! I knew it!" said Grandma. "I was sure there would be crawling things with all that quaint thatch."

"It was just a spider," said Elizabeth's mother, but Elizabeth knew that if Grandma hadn't been there, her mother wouldn't have gone near the spider, let alone pick it up!

"Are there any more of those awful things?" asked Grandma.

"No, no! That was just an odd one that came in from outside," answered Mother.

"It probably has a husband up there, too!" suggested Grandma.

"I don't think so," said Dad. "As I understand it, they eat their husbands!"

Grandma fell silent, but you could tell by the anxious way that she kept looking around that she was still thinking of spiders. After several cups of tea she was a little reassured, but she wasn't keen to go upstairs to bed. She reasoned that the upstairs rooms were nearer the thatched roof, and she was convinced that the straw was infested with spiders.

The next morning Grandma and Grandpa were downstairs before Elizabeth left for school. Grandma had lost some of her well-pressed look.

Before breakfast was even started, they began questioning her father about his work. Usually Mr. Fenner disappeared behind the morning paper for the whole duration of breakfast, and Elizabeth had been given to understand that there was an extra commandment that went, "Thou shalt not speak at breakfast."

However, Grandma either didn't know, or didn't care, about fundamental rules like that.

"Now we don't want to keep you from your work," said Grandma. "You're not to take any time away from your research on account of us. In fact, this might be a good opportunity for you to get ahead. We could take Elizabeth away somewhere for a few days. What a treat to explore these quaint villages with Elizabeth as our guide!"

"Maybe we could go to the coast," Grandpa suggested. "Elizabeth likes the sea."

After a great deal more talk, it was settled that Grandma and Grandpa would take Elizabeth to stay

at the Red Lion Inn at Merston for a day or two.
This would give Mother and Dad a chance to do lots
of writing and, Elizabeth suspected, it would put
some distance between Grandma and the creepy-
crawly thatch. She noticed that Grandma had, very
casually, asked about the age of the Red Lion Inn.
She had been told it was a lovely old place, some two
hundred years old, with a slate roof. She had then
asked if there were any modern hotels.

"Two hundred years old *is* modern in this part of
England," Elizabeth's father had replied, shortly.

It was then that Elizabeth noticed that the hands
of the grandfather clock were sneaking around toward nine o'clock, and she left for school in a noisy
swirl of coat and books and schoolbag.

That evening after school, Mother, Dad, the
grandparents, and Elizabeth drove down to the Red
Lion for supper. They followed five miles of winding roads and then dropped down into the village
nestled close to the sea.

It probably hasn't changed since Ann came here
to help in the inn, thought Elizabeth. It could have
been this very inn that her uncle owned. There
didn't appear to be any other. This thought made
Elizabeth feel ever so slightly uneasy, but she soon
forgot the feeling when she sat down at the table.

After dinner an old man joined them and began
telling tales of ghosts and hauntings of long ago. Sit-

ting in the paneled dining room, beside a bright fire, surrounded by friends, Elizabeth found it pleasantly scary.

"Did you notice the big hill behind the hotel?" the old man asked, sucking noisily on his pipe. "On a night such as this you can hear the Roman legions marching up over the brow of the hill."

"Roman legions?" asked Mr. Fenner.

"Aye, a whole Roman army, in all their fine battle dress, came marching over that hill many years ago," continued the old man.

"Where were they going?" asked Elizabeth.

"It was where they went that matters." The old man shook his head. "The mist came down, and they lost their way and went hurtling over the cliff and drowned in the sea. But, on a night like this, you can hear them marching still. Just the sound of their marching feet."

Everybody listened.

The wind wailed around the house, and it seemed to Elizabeth that, if the wind would only drop a little, she would be able to hear quite distinctly the rhythm of the marching feet. The wind rose to a scream, and it sounded like the frightened cry of the soldiers as they stepped off into black nothingness and found only the cruel rocks and the waiting sea below. Elizabeth shivered and enjoyed being frightened in the noisy comfort of the dining room.

"Time for bed," said Mother. "Dad and I are leaving now. We'll come for you on Sunday night."

To reach her bedroom Elizabeth had to go out the front door and around to a side door which opened to the rooms at the back of the inn. She paused for a moment outside and could smell the salt of the sea. Above her, partly hidden by mist was Bindon Hill. Were there really ghosts up there? Were there ghosts anywhere?

She wondered again, as she'd wondered before, about Ann. Was she a ghost or just a trick of time? She belonged to long ago, but for Elizabeth she was part of the here and now. Did that make her a ghost? Elizabeth didn't know. If she could only talk to Ann. In all their meetings she had never, as Elizabeth, talked to Ann. She had just been Ann.

Once inside the inn again, Elizabeth climbed a narrow stairway. Her bedroom was at the head of the stairs, and her grandparents had the room next door. She washed quickly and climbed into bed. She was almost asleep when Grandma looked in to see that she was settled for the night.

Some time later Elizabeth awakened suddenly and looked around the unfamiliar room. There was enough moonlight to pick out the heavy dressing table and big wardrobe. Then she heard the far away beat of a distant drum. Or was it the rhythm of marching feet? Of course, that was it! The soldiers were marching over Bindon Hill.

Cautiously, Elizabeth climbed out of bed and crept over to the window. She couldn't see the hill from there, but something else arrested her attention. Down in the small garden behind the inn stood Ann. Her shawl was pulled up over her head, and she gazed up at Elizabeth's window. When she saw Elizabeth, she smiled and waved.

This time Elizabeth felt only excitement. This could be her chance to talk to Ann. She wouldn't "become" Ann. She'd only talk to her and find an answer to all the things that had been puzzling her earlier. So she slipped on her shoes, pulled on her jacket over her pajamas, and quietly crept out of the room, and down the back stairs.

The back door wasn't even locked and opened easily when Elizabeth lifted the latch and pushed. Outside there was a snatching wind, and Elizabeth shivered and hurried around the corner of the building. Yes, there was Ann waiting for her, and Elizabeth ran to her eagerly.

Before Elizabeth could speak Ann reached out to her, and as always before, there was again only Ann in the garden. Elizabeth struggled to retain her own identity, but the present slipped away. The inn changed very little, and even the chrysanthemums and michaelmas daisies in the border appeared the same, though slightly rearranged.

Ann walked around toward the front of the house, and somewhere within her Elizabeth hoped that when she went into the inn she would find Grandma and Grandpa and the old man who had told them ghost stories.

Ann opened the door and only Ann saw the noisy crowd inside the inn. Only Ann bit her lip and clenched her fists as she pushed her way through the hot, smoky, rancid room looking for Uncle Matthew.

≫ 11 ≪
The Lucky Bonnet

Ann hated the inn at night, especially on Friday nights. It was always more crowded and noisy then. Most of the men ignored her, but occasionally they would tease her. Then she would stand, hot and embarrassed and much too shy to answer her tormentors, until Uncle Matthew told her to get back through to the kitchen.

Aunt Jenny beckoned to her from the kitchen and told her to take a tray of supper up to the guest in the back bedroom. Ann took the tray and carefully maneuvered it through the crowded room. When she reached the door, she failed to notice a young fellow sprawled on a bench with his foot across the doorway. Ann stumbled against it, and the tray tipped, sending the hot mutton pie and mug of ale crashing to the floor.

This was greeted with great laughter, but above it, she could hear Uncle Matthew scolding and telling her to get that mess cleaned up. Wearily, she fetched a bucket and cloth and finally another tray of supper.

This time she got safely outside, then back in the side door and up the stairs to the guest's bedroom. Her timid knock was answered, and she went into the room.

The man occupying the room was a gentleman. Ann could tell that by his fine clothes and his voice when he spoke.

"Let me help you," he said, taking the tray from her and setting it down on a small table.

"Sit down for a minute, child," he said. "I've been alone with my thoughts all day. Sit down and talk to me."

Ann sat down timidly. She did not want to stay, but she was much too shy to go. She was also too shy to talk.

The fine gentleman broke off a piece of the mutton pie and put it on a side plate.

"Share my supper," he said. "There's far too much for me."

Even Ann's shyness did not keep her from taking the plate of food and eating hungrily. She wiped her mouth with the back of her hand, and then her hands on her dress when the last mouthful was gone.

The man asked her questions, and gradually she found herself talking to him. She told him about her life in the cottage and helping Uncle Matthew at the inn. She even told how she had spilled his supper and the men had laughed and she'd had to get him another tray. He asked if she had ever been to school, and she hung her head and said that she could not read or write.

Suddenly, aware that he, too, had finished his supper, she jumped to her feet.

"I must go, sir. Aunt Jenny will be after me!"

"I suppose you must," he said. "I learned a lot from talking to you, child."

How could that be, Ann wondered. How could a gentleman like that learn anything from a cottage girl like her? But even more bewildering was that he reached out and placed a shiny shilling in her hand.

"Oh, no, sir!" said Ann.

"Oh, yes!" said the gentleman, with a smile, and opening the door, he gently pushed her out and handed her the empty tray.

Ann scuttled back to the kitchen, but neither Aunt Jenny nor Uncle Matthew seemed to notice she'd been gone. Each must have thought she had been helping the other. She busied herself washing mugs until Aunt Jenny told her to run off to bed.

Ann slept in a little room by the kitchen. She missed Mary and Fanny and shivered under the blankets. The room by the kitchen was warm enough and the blankets were thick, but she wished she could snuggle in beside her little sisters.

Aunt Jenny and Uncle Matthew had no children

of their own, and they were always kind to Ann when she came to help. She knew that soon she was expected to go and live with them and work in the inn. There just wasn't room for all of them at home, and she was ten years old. Old enough to work.

She liked it well enough at Aunt Jenny's because Aunt Jenny had nice things—pretty dishes and plenty of food. There was a pump right in the kitchen. But there were always too many strangers around the inn, and few of them spoke to her as kindly as the man had that night. Also, she missed the little ones dreadfully, and they'd be missing her.

By now she wanted them so badly that she could not sleep. She'd ask Aunt Jenny if she could go home tomorrow. She just had to get back to the cottage. She must go home.

Very early in the morning Ann awakened to the sound of Aunt Jenny raking the ashes in the grate. Ann pulled on her clothes and went into the kitchen to help with the morning chores.

"Can I go home today, Auntie?" Ann asked.

Aunt Jenny got up slowly from her knees and wiped her dusty hands on the skirts of her thick homespun dress. She pushed her hair back from her forehead leaving a streak of soot.

"Well, I don't know, lass. Uncle Matthew isn't going to town today, and he wouldn't want to go over Waterberry way just to take you home."

"Could I walk, then?" asked Ann.

"I dare say you could," answered Aunt Jenny. "I'll miss you, though. I was hoping you'd stay longer. You're a handy girl for all you're so little and small."

"I like it here, Aunt Jenny. But I do miss little Michael, and I just feel I must be getting home."

"All right then, lass. But you'll come again soon."

Later in the morning, when Ann was throwing the dishwater out the back door, she saw Uncle Matthew over at the coach house. He grabbed Dinty by the forelock and led her out into the yard and harnessed her to the waiting trap.

"I hear you want to go home, Ann," he called out. "There's no need for you to walk. I have to go over to Springfield Manor this morning anyway."

Not ten minutes later, Ann had given Aunt Jenny a quick kiss, and with her few extra belongings bundled into her shawl, she was perched beside Uncle Matt in the trap.

"Giddy-up, Dinty!"

With a rattle of harnesses and wheels and the echo of Dinty's hooves on the cobbled courtyard, they were off.

They wound steeply out of the village and were soon bowling along the dirt road between high hedges. It was a beautiful autumn morning. There was still a coldness in the air, but it would be warm later. The birds sang in the hedgerows and flashed across the road in front of the trotting pony. They passed cottages, and children sat on the walls and watched them go by. Ann felt as grand as the Queen of England.

Fleetingly, she wondered why she wanted to go home. She could stay with Uncle Matthew and ride in the trap and act like a fine lady every day, yet here she was in a hurry to get back to the crowded cottage and be one of the peasant children leaning over the walls, watching. She wondered if the Queen of England ever wished she was a cottage child. She didn't suppose so.

Presently they reached the village of Lower Waterberry. The men were still working on the school building at the edge of the village. Ann could have run home from here by the path through the woods, but she was enjoying the ride, and now that she was so close to home there was less urgency about getting there.

When they reached the cottage, the children came running out at the sound of the trap, and Ann scarcely waited for Dinty to stop before jumping down and running to greet them.

"Aren't you going to say good-by, lass?" asked Uncle Matthew.

"I'm sorry, Uncle! Good-by and thank you! I'll come again soon. Really, I will."

Then Ann eagerly took little Michael from her

mother's arms and sat down in the doorway holding
him. He was fretting, as he did much of the time,
and his little face was pinched. She nuzzled close to
him, and gradually his whimpering stopped and he
fell asleep in her arms.

It was good to be home again.

That same afternoon Mrs. Featherby from Springfield Farm stopped at the cottage. She was going to
Dorchester Market and wanted Willy to come along
and sell some chickens for her. But both Willy and
Thomas were out in the potato field, so it fell to Ann
to go with her.

Mrs. Featherby felt it was well below her dignity
to haggle over the price of chickens in the market
place. She also had a shrewd notion that the ragged
little Lauden children were good vendors. There
were enough people in Dorchester who were comfortable themselves and were a little moved by the
plight of the poor.

Ann would sell the chickens all right, thought
Mrs. Featherby. The child was looking unusually
frail. Some of her summer tan had faded, and her
face looked pale under the masses of tangled black
hair.

Before Ann climbed into the carriage, she turned
and ran into the house. She had hidden her coin in

one of Fanny's hiding places under a loose board in a corner of their room. She hadn't expected to have a chance to spend it so soon.

Now, seated beside Mrs. Featherby, Ann marveled at the idea of two carriage rides in one day. All too soon they reached Dorchester and the bustling market. Mrs. Featherby told Ann to get down with the basket of chickens, and with a flick of the whip she was gone.

Ann stood at the edge of the road with the basket at her feet. She hoped someone would buy one soon. Just then a large, important-looking lady sailed toward her. She was the head cook in the household of Mr. Basil, a leading businessman in Dorchester. She thought that no one was her equal when it came to preparing meals. Tonight Mr. Basil was having company, so nothing but the best would do. She questioned Ann about the chickens and then told Ann to bring them along. She'd buy all six.

She walked off up the street, and there was nothing for Ann to do but follow with the hamper of chickens. It wasn't easy. The basket would have been hard for a man to manage, and Ann was small for her ten years. People jostled and pushed, an excited dog started yapping at the basket, and the chickens scrabbled and squawked.

Fortunately, Ann was able to keep the cook in sight. She turned down an alley leading to the back door of one of the big Main Street houses. Here she paid Ann and told her to give the poultry to a loose-mouthed boy.

With a grab and a twist and a snap, each of the noisy chickens was reduced to a twitching heap of feathers. Ann didn't like the way he smiled as he did his job.

The empty basket was easier to manage, and Ann took her time about returning to her corner of the market. For the first time in her life Ann had money to spend—the silver piece the man had given her. She knew without question what she wanted to buy. She stopped at a stall bright with cottons and gay scarves and looked eagerly at the pretty things.

"Get away from there, you brat," said an angry voice from the back of the stall, and Ann jumped away. She hadn't intended buying anything there, anyway.

Then she found an old woman who was sitting on the ground with a small basket of wares in front of her. She was working as she sat, deftly crocheting a little bonnet.

"You'll not be needing a baby's bonnet, my dear," she said to Ann, in a soft, musical voice.

"But I do," said Ann, "if I can pay."

"A lucky bonnet of soft Irish wool," said the old woman.

"A lucky bonnet?" questioned Ann.

"Yes, the girl that wears this bonnet will grow to be the bonniest child in all England," the soft voice answered.

"It's for a baby boy," said Ann.

"The finest lad in all England. Oh, it's a lucky bonnet, and it'll be a lucky lad that wears it!"

Ann looked at the soft whiteness of the fine wool and the pattern of the stitches. She held out her silver coin.

"Can I have it?" she asked.

"Yes, my dear, and I'll give you three pennies in change."

Ann took the little bonnet and the pennies and stuffed them into the bodice of her dress. Then she went back to the place where she was to meet Mrs. Featherby. Most of the stalls were packed away before Mrs. Featherby's carriage rattled into view. But Ann was so excited about the little bonnet that she scarcely noticed the long wait. How surprised her mother would be and how grand Michael would look!

It was suppertime when Ann reached home, and everyone but her father and the baby was seated at the table.

"Look, Ma! I've got a present for Michael," said Ann, pulling the soft white bonnet out of her bodice.

"Did Mistress Featherby give you that?" asked her mother.

"I bought it myself," said Ann triumphantly.

"With what?" asked her mother.

"With my money," answered Ann. "A guest at the inn gave it to me."

"Why should a guest give it to you?" asked her mother sharply.

"I carried up his supper on a tray," Ann faltered.

"Money that you earn at Uncle Matthew's should go to buy food for all of us. That's not your money to go wasting on frivolity."

"What did y' buy?" asked little Fanny.

Ann held out the white bonnet and then went over and picked little Michael up from the cradle. She sat down on the settle and carefully pulled the bonnet over his little head and tied the ribbon under his chin. The hat was too big and made his tiny face look more pinched than usual. In contrast to the whiteness of the bonnet, his shawl was matted and dirty and gray.

Quietly, Ann laid him back in his bed and handed her mother the three coppers change.

"It's a lucky bonnet, Ma," said Ann.

"He'll need more than luck, that wee one," said her mother, shaking her head sadly and tears running down her face.

The children sat around the table in shocked silence. They didn't really understand the fuss about the bonnet, and now their mother was crying.

Just then their father came home. Mother bustled to the fire to get him warm potatoes, and Ann drew a mug of ale and then took her own place at the table. She helped little Mary eat and scolded Jacob for stealing Fanny's share, and she ate her own bread and potatoes without tasting them.

Late in the night Ann crept out of the house. She followed the path through the woods, stealthily, like one of the night creatures. Surely never before had the way seemed so dark and the path so long. She fought down a rising panic as she passed the church and came to the lane to Random, and the darkness was still thick around her.

The end wall of the cottage loomed gray before her. Then she looked down and saw her heavy brown oxfords and—holy cat!—pink, flapping pajama legs. Of course! She had become Ann in the middle of the night, so it was still night when she returned.

Worse still! She should be in Merston with her grandparents. Could she just turn up in her own bed? She thought of wild explanations, such as she'd come home with her parents hidden in the back of the car. But then Grandma and Grandpa would be in a frightful state if they thought they'd lost her.

The only answer seemed to be to walk back to

Merston—now. Elizabeth didn't like the idea at all. For Ann to run about in the darkness seemed all right. But Elizabeth had never gone out after dark without her parents knowing about it. Now she had to walk five miles or so down deserted roads, wearing pajamas. Also, in her hurry to go out to meet Ann, she had thrust her feet into her shoes without putting on socks. It was lucky she had worn her jacket because it, at least, was warm and the night was cold.

She judged that it couldn't be much later than two in the morning when she started along the Merston Road below Random Cottage. She was glad when she passed the last of the houses in the village. Then she saw car lights in the distance and hid in the gateway to a field. She didn't want to risk questions from late motorists.

She walked and walked. Once a farm dog chased her for almost half a mile. She walked and walked and was sure she must be nearly there. She came to a crossroads and dimly made out, "Merston 3 miles." She couldn't believe it! She had to have walked more than two miles.

At last she came to a landmark she recognized. It was a group of old elms by a wrought iron gate. Her father had been talking about the place earlier. It was called Dagger's Gate and was the scene of a long ago murder. A woman had stabbed her husband by this gate, and to this day the woman could be seen, walking up and down under the elms, wringing her hands.

Elizabeth had asked her father if he believed in ghosts. It was a subject that fascinated her now.

Her father took the question seriously and talked about it at length.

"The past lives on in us, Elizabeth," he had said. "You're so sure that all my studies in libraries and museums are a waste of time, but it helps us understand ourselves. You needn't be afraid of wailing ghosts that haunt elm trees, but the mistakes of past generations haunt us now. And we are making decisions that will haunt the future."

"The past lives on in us. The past lives on in us." The words beat a rhythm as Elizabeth jogged down the road, and they seemed to be telling her something that was just beyond her understanding.

Then Elizabeth began to think of Ann. And with the thought came the fear that just thinking of her would be enough to bring her out of the shadows in the hedgerows. She didn't want to be Ann. She didn't want to be caught up in Ann's world. Somewhere on this dark and lonely road Ann might be waiting to take her away . . . away . . . away. . . .

Elizabeth broke into a run. She was so frightened that her mind was empty of thought. There was an ache in her side, and her feet were blistered because of those shoes without socks. But Elizabeth knew only of her need to hurry. She reached the hill above the edge of the village and looked down on the cluster of houses, with the roof of the Red Lion taller than the other buildings. There were cars parked in the street, which reassured Elizabeth that she was in the present.

When she reached the inn, she was afraid that the side door might be locked, but as was the way in these villages, there was still trust and the landlord was quite casual about locking up.

Elizabeth tiptoed up to her own room. She tossed her jacket on the bed, and it slid off the satin quilt onto the floor. She kicked off her shoes and crawled into bed and snuggled down in a deep, dreamless sleep.

When Grandma wakened Elizabeth, she climbed stiffly out of bed and hurriedly pulled on socks to hide her blistered feet.

The day stretched out ahead of her. It was too cold for more than a brisk walk along the beach, so they returned to the inn. There was a blazing fire in the dining room, and they moved a table close to it and played cards. First Rummy, and then Elizabeth taught Grandma and Grandpa War and Spit.

After lunch, Grandma said she'd have a rest, and Elizabeth surprised them by saying she thought she would lie down, too. Later she heard Grandma remarking that she couldn't get over the change in Elizabeth—where had all her energy gone? She never used to be still for a moment—and now an afternoon nap!

≫ 12 ≪
The Mushroom Meadow

Grandma and Grandpa left for London on Monday morning, and Elizabeth went back to school. It was very warm for late in October, and the children found it hard to pay attention to their lessons.

"After school I'm going to look for mushrooms in a field near the abbey," Nancy whispered to Elizabeth. "Do you want to come?"

"All right," said Elizabeth. "But I don't know one kind of mushroom from another, so you'll have to show me."

"If you girls keep whispering, you'll stay after school," Mr. Ranton warned them.

Two heads bent over their books, but neither girl was attending to the lesson. Nancy was thinking that Elizabeth was much less pushy than she had seemed at first and was hoping that this time they could get to be friends. Elizabeth was thinking that it was nice of Nancy to keep giving her another chance. This time she'd really be friends. She wanted a nice, ordinary friend like Nancy.

So the two girls set off together after school. Elizabeth knew she should check with her mother, but surely going off with Nancy was just what her mother wanted her to do. Nancy seemed to have freedom to go where she pleased after school so long as she came home for tea at five.

"We don't want to drag our school books with us," said Nancy, "So I'll show you our secret place. Only Mandy and me know about this place."

The girls turned down Abbey Road and were soon out of the village. The last house had a stone wall and a very long driveway. Nancy looked all around and then pulled Elizabeth through the gate and into the bushes behind the stone wall.

"Look, there's a loose stone that we've pulled out to make a hiding place. We keep food and stuff here," said Nancy.

"I don't see any food," said Elizabeth.

"Of course not! There's only food in it if we put it there. We ate the last food a long time ago."

"Seems a pity to leave it empty," said Elizabeth.

"We'll put our school books in it," said Nancy. "We usually put our school bags in, but we'll need them today for carrying the mushrooms."

They hid their books and then crept out to the

road again taking great precautions to see that the way was clear. Elizabeth felt that she and Nancy were truly friends now that Nancy was sharing her secret places with her. She wondered what Mandy would think but didn't say anything about it.

"You really should go out after mushrooms in the morning, early," said Nancy.

"Why?" asked Elizabeth.

"They get old soon, and besides you get them before other people do! And before cows step on them," answered Nancy.

"Are there cows in the field?"

"Yes, I expect so. You're not afraid of cows, are you?"

"Of course not," answered Elizabeth. "I'm not afraid of anything!"

And this afternoon that was true. The sun was bright and warm, and nothing could hurt her. Nancy was such an everyday companion that she completely shut out Elizabeth's excursions to Ann's world.

Some late blackberries hung on the bushes, and Elizabeth picked a handful and crammed them into her mouth. They were watery and lacked the sweetness of the September berries.

"You shouldn't eat blackberries in October," said Nancy.

She, herself, was stained purple from the berries.

"Why not?" asked Elizabeth.

"The witches have put a spell on them, that's why! Only the devil's children eat October blackberries."

Elizabeth laughed, but just the same she didn't eat any more blackberries. She decided they were tasteless.

"This way," said Nancy, and they turned into the gateway of the old abbey.

Around the ruins of the abbey the lawns were neat and smooth and green. Old foundations had been uncovered and waist high walls marked out some of the rooms and cloisters. Most of the stones were moss-covered, and ivy clung to the crumbling walls. Rooks cawed harshly from the treetops above, and behind the ruins beech trees showered their gold leaves on the ground and whispered secrets to the sky. Channels of water, choked with leaves and weeds, marked the sites of the fishponds where, centuries before, the monks had kept their trout.

The girls wandered through the grounds. It was an enchanted place. They found a nest in a crevice in a wall, abandoned since spring. They saw a little snake twist through the grass and glide away into the water all in one motion. There was a stump where a squirrel had picnicked and left its empty nutshells scattered around the table.

"My dad would like it here," said Elizabeth. "He goes for places like this."

"I do, too," said Nancy. "I like places where you can see how it used to be."

"Maybe I do, too," said Elizabeth. "I always thought the past was gone, and only what's now matters."

"We'd better go look for those mushrooms, or they'll be past," said Nancy.

"We go through here," she said, pushing through the bushes and scrambling over a fence. It was barbed wire and gave them some trouble, but they reached the field on the other side only a little scratched and disheveled.

They walked along the edge of the field, and Nancy found several mushrooms almost right away and showed Elizabeth what to look for.

"I'll move over. There's no use us both looking in the same place," Nancy said.

So Nancy moved out into the open and Elizabeth stayed nearer the woods. It was quite some time before Elizabeth found one but at last she saw something white in the grass. It was perfect—smooth and white, with pink gills underneath. Near it were two little buttons pushing through the grass. Elizabeth picked these, too.

She was so intent in her search that she didn't see Ann at first. She must have passed quite close to her. It was the sound of sobbing that made Elizabeth look back toward the woods. And there she was. A small, crumpled figure sitting at the edge of the field, crying . . .

"Please, please don't go away!" Ann said in a muffled voice. "I need you. We must be friends."

There was no quick smile, and Ann's eyes were great dark pools of sadness. Elizabeth walked over and sat down beside Ann in the long grass under the trees.

"What's wrong?" she asked.

They were talking to each other at last. Now Elizabeth could find the answer to their strange friendship. But she forgot all about solving mysteries when she heard Ann's next words.

"Little Michael . . . he died . . . he just didn't ever thrive . . . and it wasn't a lucky bonnet . . . ."

Elizabeth turned and threw her arms around Ann to give her comfort and to take comfort, too, for she had loved little Michael. And then, as always happened when they touched each other, they merged into one, and only Ann lay sobbing on the grass, but within her Elizabeth cried too.

Poor little Michael. He had been so little and so frail, and he'd been theirs for such a short time.

Ann lay on the grass and sobbed and cried until she felt the chill mist from the river swirl around her. She picked herself up and stumbled home. Her throat was dry and her head hurt.

When she reached home, all the family was there.

Her mother saw her tear-stained face and came and laid a hand on Ann's rough hair.

" 'Twas nice that ye gave him the little bonnet, Ann. 'Twas right he should have had something nice of his own."

"It was supposed to be a lucky bonnet, Ma," said Ann, the tears flowing again.

"You can't buy luck, Ann," said her mother. "Michael didn't thrive, Ann, and when he got the fever yesterday, he hadn't a chance."

Later that night, lying close to little Mary, Ann's throat hurt and the coughing never stopped. She was hot, and her head throbbed, and oh, it hurt so much to cough.

I must get away from here, she told herself. I'll go away and never come back. She rose shakily from the bed and stumbled down the stairs and out into the dark night. It was cold and it hurt to breathe, yet she ran through the dark woods. She ran past the church, and her head pounded. Little stabs of light exploded before her eyes.

At last she was on the lane, and she could see Random Cottage sitting snug on its hilltop. Light spilled out from the front window. She was home at last, and the nightmare was over.

Her head still hurt, and she clung for a moment to

the door handle as a spell of shivering shook her whole body. She felt wretched. She felt so miserable and ill that Ann and her troubles were banished from her thoughts. Ann and the poor baby Michael were gone now. It was her own throbbing head that mattered.

She pushed open the door and stumbled in, calling for her mother.

But who was sitting by the fire? Where were the red chairs and the round oak table? Where were the books and newspapers? She looked around wildly. Nothing belonged. Least of all the old woman by the fire.

It was Old Scrubber Liz.

Somehow, somehow, instead of finding her way home, she had arrived at the old witch's house. Then the realization came that she was indeed home, home in Random Cottage, but this time she had not found her way back from nowhere. She was still in Ann Lauden's world, and there was no other way home.

Elizabeth wanted to turn and run, but her legs were heavy as stone. The room swam before her eyes, and she slumped down on the flagstone floor in a faint.

Scrubber Liz had been as startled by Elizabeth's entrance as Elizabeth herself. She had been frightened too, and her first instinct had been to drive the child from the house. But the girl was obviously ill and unable to go anywhere, so the old woman crossed the room and helped her over to a chair by the fire. She wrapped a shawl around her and stirred up the fire, because the strange girl was shivering so much.

Elizabeth opened her eyes and gradually the room came into focus. It was not exactly like their own sitting room, but there were things she recognized. The old grandfather clock stood solidly in its corner, and the moon faces and wind with puffing cheeks were only a little clearer. The drop-leaf table under the window was the very same, too. But the fireplace was different. Instead of the small tile fireplace with its little mantelpiece was a huge, black stove set into the wall. A big black pot hung over the fire from a hook, and a kettle simmered at the side.

A narrow stone stairway wound up by the chimney. Elizabeth looked around for the wooden stairway of their own home, but it wasn't there. Scrubber Liz noticed her move and came forward slowly and handed her a steaming mug. It smelled of spices and herbs that Elizabeth could not identify. She drank it cautiously.

Old Scrubber Liz drew up a chair at the other side of the fire and looked at Elizabeth intently.

"Well, who are you, child?" she asked. "And why do you keep coming to my house?"

"I'm Elizabeth Fenner, ma'am," said Elizabeth, and didn't know how to answer the other question.

"Elizabeth. That's my name, too, though they all call me Scrubber Liz on account of the brushes I sell. Why do you come, Elizabeth Fenner? I've seen you many times."

"I don't understand, ma'am."

"Neither do I! Neither do I!" said the old woman, shaking her head. "Sometimes when I'm here alone, I see you walk in and hang your coat behind the door and throw your books on the windowsill for all the world as if you belonged here, and then you fade away."

Elizabeth sat silent.

"I saw you in the lane once. And in the woods. You remember that?" Old Liz asked sharply.

"Yes, ma'am. You chased me. But I don't know about coming to your house. You see *I* live here too."

The words seemed to create a great chasm of mistrust, and Scrubber Liz pushed her chair back as if she were retreating from Elizabeth.

"What have you got in that bag?"

Elizabeth still had her schoolbag strapped across her shoulder.

"It's just my school books."

"You can read? Let me see the books."

Elizabeth opened her bag and instead of her reading and arithmetic books there were only three limp mushrooms. Of course! She had hidden the books in the wall and had been using the bag for collecting mushrooms. It all seemed so long ago.

Elizabeth saw the distrust deepen in Scrubber Liz's face.

"You're a witch, aren't you? You put spells on people," Scrubber Liz said softly.

Scrubber Liz, of all people, calling her a witch!

"I am not! You know yourself that just gathering mushrooms doesn't make you a witch."

"What do you know about Ann Lauden?" Old Liz asked harshly.

"I come to see her," whispered Elizabeth.

"Aye, and she comes here to find you. I see her waiting here all the time."

Then Scrubber Liz got up and stood over Elizabeth looking more fierce and frightening than ever.

"You'll not harm her. Do you hear? You'll not harm that child."

"Oh, no, ma'am," gasped Elizabeth, shrinking back in her chair. "I'll do her no harm."

The old woman leaned over her, and Elizabeth closed her eyes and pushed back against the chair. The room was going around again, and voices thundered in her ears and then tinkled with a sound of faraway bells. Faces, blurred faces, came and went. Sometimes Old Scrubber Liz peered down at her. Sometimes her own mother's hand rested lightly on her brow. Sometimes her father, sounding gruff and anxious, hovered near. Other people whom she did not know floated in and out of her consciousness.

Then Elizabeth slept.

≫ *13* ≪
The Shawl

Elizabeth slept a deep, exhausted sleep. Then she reached a state when she was not sure whether she was awake or dreaming. The door opened softly, and she heard pattering footsteps crossing the floor.

She looked up and saw Ann looking down at her. This was a smiling Ann with all the sadness gone from her eyes. She had a sweet, cheeky little face that reminded Elizabeth of a pert round robin that had hopped into the kitchen one day. Ann came close to Elizabeth, and then . . . she wasn't there. Elizabeth could still feel her presence in the room, but she could no longer see her. Then Elizabeth drifted back to sleep—if, indeed, she had been awake.

The wind blew a spatter of rain against the window, and Elizabeth awakened. Inside, the house was quiet. She looked around the room. She was back upstairs in her own bedroom, and all the reassuring, familiar things were there. The class picture of the children at Timberhill School was propped against the mirror. Her diary, with only one page filled, lay beside it—and how much she could have written!

One new feature in the room was a great array of medicine bottles and glasses on the bedside table. They must really have been worried about her.

Then Elizabeth noticed the shawl.

Lying on the floor beside the bed was the tattered brown shawl that Ann had so often worn around her thin little shoulders. Elizabeth reached down and picked it up. The wool was damp.

So it hadn't been a dream. Ann had been here. In a flash, Elizabeth understood. Ann had made a choice, too. She had left the past and would be with Elizabeth always now. What was it Elizabeth's father had said? The past lives on in us. Ann would live on in Elizabeth and would know the reading and writing she had yearned for, and Elizabeth would be a little changed too, because she had known Ann.

A door rattled across the hallway. Elizabeth stuffed the shawl into her bed and waited. Her mother's footstep sounded on the landing, and then the door opened.

"Elizabeth," said her mother. "Oh, Elizabeth, darling! How do you feel?"

"All right, Mother."

Her mother stood looking at her.

"You gave us such a fright! What happened?"

"I don't really know," answered Elizabeth cautiously. "What did happen?"

"You came home from school so late and so sick. You just didn't talk sense and didn't seem to know any of us. Then Nancy turned up with your books, worried because you'd just disappeared, when the moment before you'd been picking mushrooms with her. She couldn't understand it, and neither could I."

Mr. Fenner came in, and the worry lines relaxed from his face when he saw Elizabeth sitting up in bed talking to her mother.

"How's the mystery patient?" he asked.

"All right, I guess," answered Elizabeth, wondering how much she should tell her parents.

"Do you remember anything?" asked her father.

"Not about . . . being sick," answered Elizabeth.

"About Scrubber Liz?" asked her father.

"Scrubber Liz!" said Elizabeth.

"Now, Charles," said Mrs. Fenner sternly. "We'll talk later. You're not to question her about that now."

"What about Scrubber Liz?" asked Elizabeth, and her voice turned a little shrill.

"We're not to excite her," warned Mrs. Fenner.

"But what about Scrubber Liz?" demanded Elizabeth.

Mr. Fenner drew a chair up near the bed.

130

"We'll talk about it later. It's just that you kept saying her name last night and seemed to think your mother was Scrubber Liz. The curious thing about that was that yesterday I was reading about Scrubber Liz in the archives. She was quite a character from all accounts. She lived about a hundred years ago, and some thought she was a gypsy and some thought she was a witch. At any rate, she used to tend the sick in these parts.

"The strange thing is that she lived in this very house. This was her cottage. So when you came stumbling in and saw Scrubber Liz making you tea, it puzzled us, to say the least. But your mother's right. We won't talk of it now."

Before Elizabeth could answer, there was a knock at the front door downstairs.

"That will be the doctor, Charles. Can you let him in?"

"The doctor?" asked Elizabeth.

"Don't you remember?" said her mother. "He was here for most of the night. He said he'd be back this morning. Let me straighten your bed before he comes up."

Elizabeth clutched the brown wool shawl under the covers in a panic. If her mother straightened the bed, she'd see it and there would be questions. She wasn't ready for questions yet. Nobody must see the shawl.

"Mother, get me a glass of milk."

"In a minute, dear. You must see the doctor first."

"I want a glass of milk now! Please!"

Elizabeth was getting flushed and excited, and her mother felt she must keep her calm at all costs. So with an uncertain shrug, she said, "All right, dear! I'll get it. Now, don't excite yourself."

Immediately her mother left the room, Elizabeth jumped out of bed and stuffed the shawl into a drawer under her school clothes. She'd find a better place later. She was surprised to find that the hurried moving made her head swim, and she felt faint. She really was ill. She struggled back into bed and lay back on the pillows.

Her mother came in with the milk, followed by her father and a genial-looking doctor.

"Is it all right if she has a glass of milk?" her mother asked the doctor.

"I don't think I want it right now," said Elizabeth. She felt rather sick from the effort of getting out of bed.

Her mother looked more puzzled than angry.

The doctor took her temperature and her pulse and knocked his hammer on her knees. He peered at her throat and ears and prodded and poked and listened. Her parents watched his every move with great anxiety but could tell nothing, because all he said was, "Uh-uh," to each test and occasionally, "Good girl."

132

Then the three adults retreated to a corner of the room and talked earnestly. Elizabeth lay back on her pillows and didn't even try to listen. They wouldn't find the answer in the medical books because they were missing all the important clues.

Like the shawl.

Elizabeth got tired of thinking about Ann and Scrubber Liz, and before the doctor and her parents had finished talking, she was sound asleep.

"The best medicine of all," said the doctor, nodding toward Elizabeth, and they all tiptoed from the room.

Later in the morning Elizabeth awoke refreshed. Although her parents, and even the doctor, doubted that she could be well again so soon, she was allowed to get dressed and come downstairs.

Her parents hovered around her anxiously and made several attempts to draw her into conversation.

"The doctor thinks that maybe something has been worrying you," said her mother.

"Like to talk about it?" asked her father.

Elizabeth was pursuing a thought of her own.

"There used to be an old-fashioned fireplace here. Do you see how they have bricked it in so that this wall is about six feet deep? And look! You can see where steps used to go up to the bedrooms."

Mr. Fenner was interested at once.

"You're right, you know. I had figured out about the fireplace, but not the stairs. Now, how would you see that?"

"Could you show me the book about Scrubber Liz?" asked Elizabeth.

"Of course," answered her father. "I just never thought you cared about that sort of thing. But I'll be glad to. Maybe you could take a day off school, and we'll go in to the museum in Dorchester."

"About school," broke in her mother, trying to get the talk back to Elizabeth's worries. "Maybe we should just forget about school here. You could study at home."

Elizabeth was horrified.

"I must go to school," she said.

She remembered Ann who hadn't had the chance to go.

"I want to go. And everything will be all right now. I promise!"

≽ 14 ≼
Back to Nowhere

Elizabeth returned to school the following week and found she was quite a celebrity. Somehow or other, word had got around that Elizabeth had seen the ghost of an old woman who had lived in her cottage a hundred years ago. There were various versions of the story. Some said Elizabeth had been sick because she'd seen the ghost of a witch. Some said she'd been sick and been cured by a witch. Everyone wanted to hear Elizabeth's own account. But she wouldn't say much, so they stuck to their own more exciting stories.

Strangely enough, the person most impressed by the ghost story was Mandy. She put aside her unfriendly manner and made a real effort to be nice to Elizabeth. She didn't question her about Scrubber Liz at all. She just let Elizabeth know she wanted to be friends. She shared a chocolate bar during break and chose Elizabeth first for her team in rounders.

Nancy was glad that Mandy no longer snubbed Elizabeth because she liked them both and, until now, had to choose to be with one or the other. Now that they were all friends she had a big plan ready.

The three girls were huddled in a corner of the cloakroom, sharing an apple. They were supposed to be playing in the playground because it wasn't raining. The rule was that on dry days you played outside. However, it was worth taking a chance breaking the rule, because here they had a quiet corner.

"Let's have a Guy Fawkes party," suggested Nancy.

"A what?" asked Elizabeth.

"Don't you have Guy Fawkes night in America?" asked Mandy.

"Of course, they wouldn't," said Nancy. "It was the English parliament he blew up."

"Why do you have a party if he blew up parliament?" asked Elizabeth. "Was it a bad parliament?"

"No," said Mandy. "He didn't blow it up. He just planned it. So we let off fireworks, and then we burn him in a bonfire. We have to make a Guy and throw him in the fire."

"I know about the Guy," said Elizabeth. "I saw some little boys with a scarecrow thing, and they were saying, 'A penny for the Guy! A penny for the Guy!'"

"Yes," said Mandy. "Then they spend the money on fireworks."

Mandy and Nancy decided that this would be a

Guy Fawkes night for Elizabeth to remember. In the end, their whole families were invited. This was partly because there would be more money for fireworks that way and mostly because their parents wouldn't hear of them letting off fireworks by themselves.

The party was to take place on Guy Fawkes night, the fifth of November, and it was going to be held at the edge of the field next to Random Cottage. This place had been chosen because there was already quite a pile of hedge clippings and prunings ready for a bonfire. The girls had got permission to drag dead branches from the woods behind to add to the pile.

Mr. and Mrs. Fenner were delighted that Elizabeth was at last involved in something. The project appealed to them because it was tied up with history, and as usual, Mr. Fenner was telling Elizabeth a great deal more than she needed to know about Guy Fawkes and the times he lived in. He had planned to blow up the House of Lords and King James I as well. He was King James VI of Scotland, which sounded confusing to Elizabeth. All this had happened—or rather had not happened—on the fifth of November in 1605, and poor Guy Fawkes was still being punished for his sins. It seemed unfair to Elizabeth, but she was willing to perpetuate the tradition.

Her parents were so enthusiastic about the party

that they offered to serve hamburgers and coke, which probably wasn't traditional at all, but everybody thought it sounded good.

They liked all the comings and goings that the planning involved and enjoyed feeling annoyed with Elizabeth for talking too long on the phone. It was so long since they'd had that complaint.

First, Elizabeth, Nancy, and Mandy made the Guy. Mrs. Fenner had found a very mildewed old raincoat in the garage, which she was certain could be of use to no one. Mandy, who had an assortment of brothers, was able to bring some old jeans and a shirt, and they stuffed them with newspapers. Gradually Guy Fawkes took shape, and they became quite fond of him.

The next job was to get wood for the fire. They found that it was quite hard work to carry the dead branches from the woods to add to their pile. It was the day before the party, and they struggled with the last load. A thin, gray drizzle of rain was falling, but the girls were warmly dressed and too full of excited plans for the next day to care about the weather.

Dragging their branches, they cut through a corner of the old graveyard. The stones were crooked and moss-covered, and the grass was rough.

"I wonder how old these graves are," said Elizabeth.

"It will say the dates on the gravestones," said

Nancy, and the girls paused by a small, plain stone.

The writing was completely hidden by moss and lichen, but Nancy knelt down and peeled it off to expose the faintly chiseled letters. The light was poor, and she spelled out the writing slowly.

ANN LAUDEN

10 JUNE 1861 – 20 OCTOBER 1871

"Ann Lauden," repeated Elizabeth softly. "Is there no other name?"

"That's all I can make out. She'd be just about our age."

The girls were quiet for a few minutes as they went back to the task of pulling the branches along the path. But by the time they reached the bonfire, Nancy and Mandy were chattering again about the party.

"That should be enough," said Nancy, heaving her wood onto the pile.

"It has to be," answered Mandy. "It's time we went home. It's almost dark."

Elizabeth said good-by to Mandy and Nancy absent-mindedly. She stood, undecided, in the fading evening light, watching them run down the lane to the village. Then she turned abruptly and took the path back to the graveyard.

Kneeling by the grave she traced the letters with her fingers. The twentieth of October. The night she had been so ill. The night poor Ann had been so ill. The last time Ann had come to her.

Ann was with her now. She was sure of that. And then came a disquieting thought. Always, for Elizabeth to find her own place and time, she had followed the path from the cottages back to Random. Might the reverse be true, also?

For Ann to get back to *her* place and time then Elizabeth must go back to the cottages. It was as simple as that.

She tried to push the idea away. She told herself that the moss-covered stone was surely proof that it was all over. But she knew that what was really holding her back was the thought that if Ann found her own time again, where would that leave Elizabeth?

She didn't have to go to the cottage tonight, she told herself. Some other time would do. She could just run home to Random now. The thought of Random brought back the memory of Old Scrubber Liz. What was it that Scrubber Liz had said? "You'll not harm her! Do you hear? You'll not harm Ann Lauden."

Elizabeth got up stiffly and began her last journey to nowhere. The woods were dim and quiet—and waiting. She walked down the path and took the right fork, deeper into the wood. She walked slowly at first, and then she began to run, because it would soon be completely dark. She pushed her way through a clump of dead, brown bracken at the edge of the clearing and then stood looking at the cottages.

There they were, in the very last light of the day, even more derelict than when she had first seen them.

The adventure was over.

She turned toward home. Somewhere along the path she stumbled over a smooth, round stone. She looked again—it wasn't a stone. It was the old jar, completely empty, and partly covered with moss and dirt as if it had lain there a long, long time. She picked it up and carried it with her.

Dinner was on the table when she reached home, but she still needed a few minutes alone before she could take up the threads of everyday life and everyday chatter.

She ran up to her room and lifted up a corner of the mattress. She pulled out a paper package and carefully unwrapped it, revealing the old, ragged brown shawl. She fingered the coarse wool and knew that Ann was with her.

"Elizabeth! Dinnertime!"

"Coming, Mother," she answered.

Elizabeth put the shawl back in its hiding place. Someday she might tell someone all about it. Someday. But not yet.

Margaret Anderson is a biologist with a penchant for writing.

Born and educated in Scotland, she received a Bachelor of Science degree from the University of Edinburgh and has worked as a biologist and statistician in England, Canada, and at Oregon State University in Corvallis.

Her science and nature articles have appeared in many children's magazines, and an article on caddis flies, co-authored with her husband, won the Canadian Entomological Society's 1973 writers competition award. She is also the author of *Exploring the Insect World* (McGraw Hill, 1974).

In 1972 Margaret Anderson and her family spent a sabbatical year in England where they lived in a two-hundred-year-old cottage called "Random"— and where she was inspired to write her first novel, *To Nowhere and Back*.

She now lives in Corvallis, Oregon with her husband and four children.